The marquis s[illegible]ely new way. He pulled her close against him, and his mouth moved with greater urgency. Odd that the touch of a pair of lips could resonate throughout her body, making her fingertips tingle and causing a warm ball in her stomach to unravel and expand. Heat flowed down her arms and legs.

How was it possible to feel such fluttering yearnings when she did not trust him? How could his big hands splayed across her back make her feel secure when she was not even sure she liked him?

The moon was still a prisoner to the clouds when the marquis stepped away.

"Are you certain you can control every situation with men, Arabella. . . ?

Also by Rebecca Ashley
Published by Fawcett Books:

THE RIGHT SUITOR
A LADY'S LAMENT
A SUITABLE ARRANGEMENT
LADY FAIR
FEUDS AND FANTASIES
RUINS AND ROMANCE
AN AWKWARD ARRANGEMENT

A MISS WITH A PURPOSE

Rebecca Ashley

FAWCETT CREST • NEW YORK

A Fawcett Crest Book
Published by Ballantine Books
 Published in the United States by Ballantine Books, a division of Random House, Inc., New York, and simultaneously in Canada by Random House of Canada Limited, Toronto.

Library of Congress Catalog Card Number: 92-97266

ISBN 0-449-22088-5

Manufactured in the United States of America

First Edition: May 1993

For Marcia and Charlotte for help and support

Chapter 1

THERE HE sat, rich and handsome and overbearingly selfish.

Arabella was seated across from Lord Ridgeton in his well-appointed study. Sunlight flowed off the windowpanes like melting honey and cast a soft glow over the marquess's strong features.

"So good of you to see me, Lord Ridgeton." She smiled thinly. In truth, Arabella thought seeing her was the least the man could do. By the time this interview was over, she meant to have his promise to do a great deal more.

He inclined his head and waited.

"Have you received my messages?" She strained to remain cordial, knowing perfectly well he had received her messages. She had written at length insisting he send money for improvements at the mill. His reply had been a silly letter that did not address her demands at all.

A slow, arrogant smile touched his lips. "Yes, I received your letters, Miss Fairingdale."

She waited for him to say more. He did not. His brown eyes were velvety in appearance, like those of a tame mink she had once seen. His mouth was cut in a single line; she wondered if it stretched enough to turn up into a real smile. He might be handsome, but he was also superior and insufferable. If she had had a choice, she would not conduct business with him.

Alas, she did not have a choice.

Arabella leaned intently toward him, swiping absently at the troublesome blue satin bonnet slipping forward. "You see, Lord Ridgeton, matters are not as they ought to be in Manchester, and we are obliged to fix them. Perhaps I did not explain that fully in my letter."

He formed his fingers into a steeple and touched his lips with the blunt fingertips. He almost smiled. "Miss Fairingdale, your letter was fifteen pages long. I doubt there is anything you failed to convey in it. Except," he added, with disapproval brisk enough to make his voice harden, "your intention of coming to London."

"I did *not* intend to come to London," she said impatiently. "I had to come to speak to you about money." He sat watching her with frosty brown eyes, his arms folded across his chest as he lounged comfortably on the other side of the ship-sized desk. He did not offer money.

A less confident woman might have been rebuffed by his lack of response. Arabella, however, was not intimidated. She critically noted the expensive black boots polished to a reflective shine and the snug white unmentionables. His coat was a fine gray wool. Such clothes must cost a pretty penny. His house was the grandest in St. James's Square. Since he was as rich as a nabob, there was no reason to refuse her the fifty thousand pounds she had requested. The money could not mean all that much to him.

Arabella had no intention of leaving him in peace until she got the money. Hadn't she hung from the slender branch of a larch tree when she was eleven until Papa agreed to buy her the dappled pony? Oh, she was no longer so selfish in her desires. Now she put her strong will to better use. The crowded, dangerous mill she and Lord Ridgeton had recently inherited together was such a cause. Once it was made safe for the workers, she could turn her thoughts back to her own rather uncertain living arrangements.

"I do not wish to be gone from Manchester long, Lord Ridgeton. I should return soon to see about the operation of the mill." Arabella supposed she could be forgiven for sounding virtuous. After all, *she* was being responsible and he was not.

He sighed and put his hands atop the desk. "Miss Fairingdale, what makes you believe you are equipped to judge the managing of a textile mill? Surely you have little experience in such matters."

Arabella rose and paced the big, book-filled study. The blue gown that swung with each turn was not of the finest silk, but the color suited her well. "I may not have experience, but I can see. I witnessed things that must be corrected immediately. You will recall that I detailed them in my letter," she added pointedly. "I am not going to rest until matters are corrected." Nor, she thought darkly, was she going to let him rest.

She had spent a laborious week trying to deciper the books of the establishment, but she had little head for figures and she had soon been hopelessly befuddled. But she did know the workers were leading hard lives.

She saw the marquess watching her as if she were an outrageous character in a bad farce. He seemed amused and interested to see what she would do next, but he also seemed removed—like a patron viewing the performance from the most elegant box.

Arabella lifted her head proudly, causing the undependable bonnet to fly backward and hang from its ribbons around her neck. She left it there. His Lordship would soon realize she was not some actress from whom he could distance himself. She was his business partner, and she meant to make him aware of his duties.

The time had come to dispense with surface politeness and speak plainly. "If you had come to Manchester to see the condition of the mill, milord, you could have saved me a tedious journey."

"Miss Fairin—"

"If you had sent money to repair the building, that would have also helped." She circled past the gleaming white fireplace with its polished brass screen and kept going, blue skirts swirling. "But you have done nothing, and I have made a most uncomfortable journey here to make you aware of your obligations." She stopped to stare defiantly at him.

"Are you through, Miss Fairingdale?" The brown eyes no longer looked tame. They glinted like cold, hard onyx. His voice had grown steel-hard.

She felt a moment's hesitation before drawing herself up to her greatest possible height. "For the moment, yes."

"Then be seated." His words cracked around the room like a shot.

She sat.

"First, allow me to remind you that women are not suited to managing businesses. Secondly, Miss Fairingdale, you know nothing of trade." He fixed a cool, challenging gaze on her. Arabella could well imagine a servant might give way under such a look.

"I may not know at present, but I am willing to learn."

He dismissed that with a rough wave of his hand. "Let us be sensible. Part of the mill was bequeathed to you because my uncle, Lord Aubrey, was a friend to your father. I am certain, however, that Lord Aubrey did not intend for you to involve yourself."

"It doesn't matter what he intended. He is dead now—and part of the mill is mine." She did not mean to sound cold and callous, but she was more concerned about the living than the dead.

He sighed. "Miss Fairingdale, there is very little profit to be had from the mill. At most we might realize one or two thousand pounds a year, and you and I would have to share that. I have a better suggestion."

She watched him with suspicion. He had not responded to her letter and he had not greeted her with any warmth, so she doubted he had suddenly become magnanimous. "What is it?"

"I have decided to buy your share."

Buy her share of the mill?

Arabella bit her lip and fought temptation. It was true that only small profits were being realized from the mill. If any improvements were made, all of those profits would be turned back into the mill, leaving her with no more money than the pittance she managed on now. If it were not for the fact she had somewhere to live, she did not know how she would manage.

For the past three years, she had lived in a house on the back of the Baxter estate. After Lady Baxter's death, Arabella had remained in the house under the charity of the administrators. All that, however, might change soon. The new master of Baxter House had arrived from the American colonies. He could easily put her out or force her to pay rent. How would she manage then? And here was Lord Ridgeton offering to buy her part of the mill . . .

Arabella's integrity surfaced and she tilted her head up. She could not sacrifice the workers at the mill for her own future comfort. If she was evicted from the house, she would deal with the problem when the time came. Meanwhile, she must deal with this problem now. "No, Lord Ridgeton, I do not wish to sell."

His jaw hardened.

"I have a duty . . . and I intend to carry it through."

He studied her with interest. She did not delude herself that he was appreciating a face generally acknowledged to be pretty. Rather, he regarded her as if she were a nasty bug he might smash. "Laudable words, Miss Fairingdale," he said curtly. "Precisely how do you intend to proceed? Your letters indicated your funds are limited."

Arabella flushed. "I have no funds for the repair of the mill." She had few enough funds for her own maintenance. "I have applied to you for the money," she continued evenly. "I am not asking for a gift. Once the mill is safe and profits can again be taken, I shall repay you."

One side of his mouth slid upward in a sardonic smile. "It would take you fifty years to repay such a debt."

Arabella suspected he was right but did not say so.

All traces of humor left his face. Leaning toward her, he spoke slowly, as if addressing himself to someone who was witless. "I am not going to give you any money."

Uncaring snob, she fumed inwardly. Aloud, she said serenely, "Then I must change your mind." Arabella did not care if she was forced to remain in London all Season to bedevil him. She did not care if she had to follow him back to his overbuilt mansion in the middle of Salisbury. In short, she was prepared to hound the man. She would come to his house, and send him letters, and go to every London event he attended. She would approach him in salons and withdrawing rooms and over glasses of lukewarm punch at every ball of the Season.

He rose, indicating an end to the interview. "There seems to be nothing more to be gained here. I hope you enjoy your stay with Lady Hector," he said, with perfunctory courtesy. "She is a charming lady."

"I know." Lady Hector and Arabella's mother had been friends before Lady Hector made a suitable match with an earl and Arabella's mother made a love match with the wonderful, witty, impoverished man who had been Arabella's father.

Arabella stood and brushed at her skirts. The fabric was no longer new and it wrinkled easily under her fingertips. Ignoring that, she said, "I look forward to seeing you, milord. I've no doubt we shall meet again." And again and again. She would make a point of it.

He murmured some insincere words of parting and held the heavy oak door for her.

Emily sat waiting outside the study. Arabella bent and touched her companion's arm. "We are ready to leave."

Emily got slowly to her feet and took Arabella's arm. Her grip was becoming tighter as her sight progressively failed her. Emily's near blindness was distressing because she was so young, but she bore it with good spirit.

A footman held the front door for them.

"Well?" Emily quizzed as soon as the door had closed behind them.

"It will take a bit of persuasion, but the marquess will come round. I must see to it that he does. Too many people will suffer if he does not."

"She's five-and-twenty and has never been married." Harry Bartley stood by the large glass window and swirled the liquor in his glass so fiercely some of it spilled over the side and ran over his chubby fingers—before dripping onto the club's exquisite Oriental carpet.

"I didn't ask you to investigate Miss Fairingdale."

"I'm not going to charge you, Cedric. I did this as a favor."

"You needn't have," he said shortly. "I don't intend to have any further contact with her."

"You did inherit a mill together. Not much money in such things, but then you don't need money. She might, though."

Lord Ridgeton drained the wine in his glass and sank deeper into his chair. Devil take Miss Fairingdale. The club room was already hot, yet a servant stoked the fire energetically. For a moment the marquess's thoughts went back to a bitterly cold night in France when he would have given all he owned for such heat as this. Pushing the memory aside, he signaled for another glass of wine.

"Comely, too," Harry continued.

Both men were thirty, but Harry had not aged as well. Although he practiced regularly at Gentleman Jackson's, his body was puffy and his cheeks round and rosy. Each day he vowed to forego rich foods and sweet wine, but his willpower seldom lasted beyond midmorning.

"Miss Fairingdale is comely if one likes blond-haired chits," Lord Ridgeton muttered. He did not. Nor did he care for stormy eyes that flashed from blue to silver. She did have a rather fresh complexion of soft pinks and feather whites, but one could scarcely appreciate even that when she was so outrageous. For her to demand money was unacceptable. No other woman of his acquaintance would have made such a request.

"There are rumors she is headstrong," Harry added.

Lord Ridgeton snorted, startling the servant who had appeared with his wine. "She is an untamed filly. I pity the poor man who tries to tame her."

"Dashed odd of Lord Aubrey to leave part of a mill to a woman," Harry observed, and took the wine for himself. "I daresay he felt sorry for her because she has no money. Her mother was from a good family, but her father was an inventor. He died without leaving the family provided for. Still, the girl has a good education. Friends of the mother saw to that."

"I thought you gave up being a detective after someone broke your arm," the marquess observed.

"No one broke it," Harry said moodily. "Fell from a horse and injured m' arm."

"Ahh."

"I did! Besides, there's little danger associated in finding out the past of a respectable woman."

"I daresay not," Lord Ridgeton agreed. "I don't recall Miss Fairingdale ever being presented. I would have remembered her," he added, with a wry twist of his mouth. If she was five-and-twenty, she would have been presented long before he left to go fight Napoléon. During his salad days he had noticed all the women.

Frankly he had done more than notice. He had kissed some of the loveliest debutantes of the Season. He had dallied more seriously with a series of courtesans.

"She wasn't presented, but she had some offers

all the same. Turned down Winby and Drysdale. There was some rumor about a French nobleman who pursued her and took her for a ride in a balloon."

The marquess watched the servant return with the poker and prod the fire until the room was an inferno. He thought again of that frigid night in France. He could almost hear the men moaning and the horses stamping their feet to keep from freezing. He shoved the thought aside. The war was two months behind him. It was time to forget it and get on with his life.

"A balloon," Lord Ridgeton repeated. "What utter nonsense. It sounds like some tale Miss Fairingdale might have concocted. I suspect she is capable of inventing all sorts of stories—and making a mull of anything she lays her hands to."

The mill was a case in point. No woman of sense would have gone to Manchester, let alone tried to say how the mill ought to be managed. Men were paid to run businesses, and they knew their jobs far better than she did.

He had offered to buy her share of the mill to be rid of her. Her refusal annoyed him and was further proof that she was addlepated. Even for his mistresses, Lord Ridgeton had always selected women who were agreeable and deferred to him. The only time he wished to see passion in a woman was in the boudoir.

Harry finished his wine and stared guiltily at the empty glass. "I ought not to have drunk that." As he looked at the marquess, his expression turned resentful. "Why is your stomach flat and mine round? You haven't gained half a stone since we were at Eton together. Isn't fair."

War had not been conducive to growing fat, Lord Ridgeton reflected as he pushed himself up from the chair. He did not say it aloud because he didn't wish to talk about the war any more than he wished to remember it. "I shall be roasted alive if I remain in this room."

" 'Tis a trifle warm." A servant sailed by with another glass of wine and Harry looked longingly after it.

"I shall see you this evening at the Willoughbys'," the marquess said.

"Wouldn't miss it. It will be the event of the Season." Harry lowered his voice mysteriously. "If I am a few minutes late, do not concern yourself."

Grinning, Lord Ridgeton shook his head. "Harry, if you do not give over playing at detective, you will have your head shot off for your trouble."

"I trust I am smarter than that."

"I hope so."

Lord Ridgeton stepped out into the darkness and tucked his ebony-headed cane beneath his arm. The cool breeze felt good after the excessive heat in the room. As he started toward the smart curricle where his tiger awaited him, a peculiar-looking vehicle lumbered by. The back wheels were low and wide-set, while the front wheels were built much higher. The result was the carriage sloped backward at an odd angle. The driver sitting hunched over the reins wore a preposterous tricorn hat atop a white wig.

Who would be foolish enough to ride in such a conveyance and with such a driver?

He forgot about the vehicle as he continued onward and his thoughts turned to the Willoughbys' party. He hoped it proved a distraction. Before the war, he had enjoyed routs and gaming and dalliances with members of the demimonde.

Since his return from the war, however, nothing interested him. Until his contretemps with Arabella Fairingdale yesterday, he hadn't even felt any strong emotions.

Seed pearls adorned the bodice of Arabella's amber gown and tiny embroidered flowers with pearl centers danced across the rest of the gown. The spun silk billowed airily about her legs as she alighted from the carriage. She turned to smile back at Lady Hector. "I am terribly excited and just a bit nervous."

The countess nodded calmly, causing the white plume atop her turban to sweep up and down. Her purple striped gown revealed plump arms, cascading bosom, and thick shoulders. In spite of her weight, some of the beauty of her youth still showed in her twinkling gray eyes and ready smile. "Everyone of importance will be here. You will enjoy yourself immensely."

It was Arabella's turn to nod. She anticipated an evening of fun and perhaps even a flirtation. She wanted to laugh and whirl about the polished dance floor. Still, she reminded herself, the parties and routs were merely a way to fill her time until she convinced Lord Ridgeton of his duties.

Even her sojourn in London with Lady Hector was temporary. Although Lady Hector and Arabella's mother had been good friends, Arabella could not impose on the countess too long. As soon as the Season ended, Lady Hector would return to her house in the country and resume spoiling the half dozen grandchildren she had left behind.

All that was in the future, however. Tonight Arabella intended to immerse herself in the moment. Her excitement crept higher with each step up the wide marble staircase. As she stood waiting in line, she peeked through the open doors. "They have a mirrored ballroom," she whispered to Lady Hector. "The room is oval and looks perfectly charming."

"It has beautiful frescoes on the ceiling," Lady Hector said. "You must be sure to notice them."

Yes, she would notice every detail. Arabella had spent little time in grand houses. Although Mama had been from a wealthy family they had disapproved of Papa, and Mama's only brother, now dead, had not received them. Since the ancestral home had been entailed, upon Arabella's uncle's death it had passed to a distant male relative and she had never been inside it.

She harbored no real resentments, though. Her childhood, while unconventional, had been a happy one. She would not trade that for the grandest mansion in the realm.

Arabella stepped inside the antechamber and smelled perfume and spirits. The polished floor beneath her new kid slippers shone cheerfully up at her. Smiling she made her way down a receiving line of women draped in elegant gossamer gowns and men dressed to perfection in gleaming cravats and flawless coats.

Arabella exited into the oval ballroom with Lady Hector beside her. The countess's hair had gone white several years ago, and she had eschewed henna and dyes in favor of plumes and turbans. The large white plume on her turban bobbed about as she nodded to people she knew.

Arabella touched her own hair to make certain the tiny cluster of white feathers held firm at the knot at the back of her head. A few blond curls had already escaped to cavort about her face and she tucked one back as she scanned the crowded room. Mirrors made the big room seem twice as large and caught the glitter from the chandeliers hanging below the hand-painted ceiling frescoes. It was beautiful and impressive and she smiled her appreciation.

Lady Hector led her along offering gossip and advice. "Don't go near Sir Robert. There's Lord Hadley; he's lived in India. He's a bit of a bore. Lady Alice is a sweet little thing." She raised her voice in greeting. "Ah, Mrs. Stone. How good to see you."

Lady Hector stopped beside a group of women gathered around damask settees and chairs with slender, fluted legs. Arabella responded politely to introductions.

"I saw your . . . er . . . carriage today, Miss Fairingdale." Lady Elizabeth outlined the scallops of her fan with a long fingernail. "It is most unusual."

"My coachman in an inventor. He designed it." Mr. Wilkes and Arabella's father had worked together on many inventions before Papa's death. The aging Mr. Wilkes's true interest was in flight machines, but he also dabbled at trying to invent a carriage that did not need a horse to pull it. He had constructed Arabella's own carriage using cast-off parts from other vehicles. She knew the chaise was far from fashionable, but it would hurt his feelings if she did not ride in it. He loved to don his tricorn hat and powdered wig and drive.

Lady Elizabeth looked up from inspecting her fan. "Is the carriage comfortable?"

No. Arabella constantly worried the cab would slide off the back and spill her onto the ground. Still, she did not wish to diminish Mr. Wilkes's hard work. "I am getting used to it," she said brightly.

"I see." Lady Elizabeth's cool eyes swept over her, then seemed to dismiss her.

Arabella knew her gown was not of the first stare of fashion, but she was here and she meant to enjoy herself. With a gay smile at Lady Elizabeth, she turned to watch the couples dancing.

The musicians were in the midst of a fast-paced country set, and Arabella tapped her foot in time as couples moved and darted on the floor. She was admiring the dancers' skill when she saw Lord Ridgeton standing tall and motionless in the doorway. His dark hair was brushed close to his scalp and his legs looked like smooth pillars in gray unmentionables. He wore a dark gray coat cut away in front and dropping to tails in the back. He surveyed the room the way he might have surveyed the cattle in his stables—with a critical, proprietary air.

An indignant flush rolled over her cheeks. How arrogant he was.

The women standing near Arabella had also noticed him, and he became the subject of their talk.

"Do you suppose Lord Ridgeton will ever marry?" Lady Elizabeth wondered aloud.

"He needs a little time," Lady Hector said kindly. "He has only recently returned from the campaigns."

Lady Elizabeth beamed toward him. "Such a handsome man. Any woman would be accounted fortunate to have him as a husband."

Heads nodded all around.

Arabella pursed her lips. She thought he would be a dreadful husband. "There are certainly more agreeable men than Lord Ridgeton," she noted.

All heads swiveled toward her.

"Do you know him?" Lady Elizabeth asked with keen interest. Her gaze once again trailed down Arabella's outmoded gown.

"Yes. I spoke with him just today."

"He *called* on you?" She couldn't repress the titter of excitement in her voice.

"No, I called on him."

A long silence followed this pronouncement. The

women glanced toward one another, then quickly away.

Lady Hector took Arabella's arm and they began walking. "Let me introduce you to some more people. You must meet some young men, so that you can dance. . . . We so enjoyed talking with you," the countess called back to the bevy of dowagers.

Arabella knew she had shocked the women. Young ladies did not call on gentlemen. Well, she did not care what other young ladies did. They were here solely for the purpose of finding a husband, but she was here to make Lord Ridgeton act responsibly.

Lady Hector stopped beside a slender man. "Arabella, dear, I would like you to meet the son of a dear friend. Lord Thorton, this is Miss Fairingdale."

"How charming to meet you."

Within a few moments Arabella was gliding about the floor with Lord Thorton. He was possessed of a narrow mustache and an endearing grin that revealed a missing tooth. Next she danced with a heavy man with bright red cheeks who was named Mr. Bartley. He had confided something to her about being a detective, but she was not certain she had understood correctly. He had a tendency to glance about as if he were being followed and to mumble over his shoulder.

He danced with great energy and swung her about abruptly, setting her squarely on the toes of another man.

"Dreadfully sorry, Miss Fairingdale," he muttered.

"It doesn't signify." Well, it might to the man limping off the floor, but Arabella was fine.

"Perhaps we ought to sit down," he suggested.

Arabella nodded and Mr. Bartley escorted her to

a section of the curving wall. She sat on one end of a brocade settee whose arms curved outward as if to enfold her in an embrace. Mr. Bartley sat stiffly beside her, cupping his arms around his protruding stomach as if to hide it.

"I have heard a great deal about you, Miss Fairingdale," he blurted after a moment's silence.

"Oh? I cannot imagine how." She had not been in London long, and she had few ties to the fashionable world.

"I have my sources," he said, with a knowing wink.

What an odd man, but he seemed pleasant and harmless. She smiled at him. "I knew a Mary Bartley at school, but if she told you I put the pudding in Miss Holmes's chair, that isn't true." Not entirely anyway. Jane Moore had helped.

"I don't concern myself with sins of the past," he informed her mysteriously. "I am more interested in sins of the present."

"I'm not sinning at present." The marquess danced into view holding a lovely brown-haired woman.

Mr. Bartley leaned in closer, causing a button to pop and roll off the ball of his stomach. He took no notice. Looking intently at her, he confided, "There are those who are sinning, you may depend on it, Miss Fairingdale. London is a town of secrets and scoundrels and strange bedfellows."

"Goodness." And active imaginations, she decided. "Well, I am not here to participate in any scandal. I am visiting my mother's old friend and conducting business. All very respectable." A thought occurred to her and she looped a curl around her finger as she looked toward the marquess. "Do you know Lord Ridgeton?"

"Cedric! Good lord, yes. Known him since he was

on the playing fields at Eton. Know his mama. She hasn't come to London since her husband died three years ago. Pity. Saintly woman," he added reverently. "A pattern card of respectability."

"Is His Lordship's life as exemplary?" Arabella inquired, with a dainty little smile. She hoped Mr. Bartley didn't realize she was shamelessly trying to learn something to help in her crusade to force Lord Ridgeton into taking proper responsibility for the mill.

He hesitated. "Shouldn't like to tell tales on a friend, you understand."

"Your loyalty is commendable." But not very helpful. Arabella looked up to see the marquess moving about the dance floor with a beautiful black-haired woman. Resentment swelled within her chest. How dare he enjoy himself so freely after he had refused to help his workers? "He seems to have an eye for the ladies," she observed.

Mr. Bartley cleared his throat. "Rather a bold statement, ma'am. I should say the ladies seek out Cedric as much as he seeks them out."

Yes, women probably would overlook a good deal to gain a share of Lord Ridgeton's wealth. It did not hurt that he was handsome and solidly built. It was unfortunate that he was without charity or concern for others.

"He was in the war and performed some dashed heroic deeds. He won't talk about them, though. Modest to a fault."

"Indeed," she murmured drily. She doubted the word "modest" could be used to describe the marquess. If he didn't want to talk about the campaigns, it was either out of stubbornness or because he had nothing to brag about.

"Whenever talk turns to the war, he goes quiet. At first I thought he'd left some sweet French girl behind and was pining for her, but it wouldn't be like Cedric to pine for a woman. He moves along briskly from one to the next. Dear me, I daresay I shouldn't have said that." He rose abruptly, sheepish at having spoken too bluntly. "Let me get you some cake and punch."

Arabella would rather have heard more about the marquess, but Mr. Bartley was already scurrying through the crowd toward the refreshment table. He moved with all the determination of a small, stubborn dog in pursuit of a fast fox.

Mr. Bartley returned a few minutes later bearing the refreshments and talking as he approached. "Cake is a bit damp. I'm afraid I spilled some of the punch on it. If you'd like me to go for another piece, I will—even though the line is long."

"No, I wasn't very hungry anyway."

"Didn't think you were. One doesn't stay as slender as you by gobbling cake."

Arabella was glad when Mr. Bartley returned her to Lady Hector. By then Lord Ridgeton was in the company of a laughing redhead. Over the next hour, Arabella stood up with half a dozen men, but the marquess never once approached her. He didn't even look in her direction. She was not so foolish as to think he had failed to see her.

The man was avoiding her.

Arabella intended to change that.

Chapter 2

WHEN LORD Ridgeton left the ballroom, Arabella followed him down the hall and into a room where a card game was in progress. There he took a position behind a curling-lipped dandy and stood watching the play.

Arabella stood a moment in the doorway watching the marquess joke with the dandy and idly sweeping back hair from his forehead. She sailed up to her quarry. "Good evening, milord," she said pleasantly.

He bowed politely. "Good evening, Miss Fairingdale."

His coolness did not deter her. "There is a dreadful crowd in the ballroom. I don't wonder you didn't spy me in there."

A muscle twitched briefly at the corner of his mouth. "A dreadful crowd," he agreed.

"Not so crowded as the mill at Manchester, you understand. Some of the workers there scarcely have a place to stand."

One of the players looked up.

"I meant to make that clear in my letters, milord, but I may have failed to do so. I shudder to think what would happen in case of a fire."

Half a dozen players stared at them over their cards.

"The air is so bad one can hardly stand to

breathe. It is thick and oppressive and full of the smell of some sort of—"

"Miss Fairingdale, I find it hot in here." Smiling urbanely he took her arm. To the casual observer it might have looked like an innocent gesture, but she felt iron fingers snap over her arm. "Some cool air would be refreshing," he added as he steered her out of the room.

Arabella did not resist. It was part of her plan to get him alone and explain in precise detail about the problems at the mill. He marched her out of the room and down the hall, moving so fast she was half pulled off her feet.

As soon as they reached the balcony, he released her arm and wheeled to face her. "What the devil did you think you were doing in there?"

"I was—"

"You were trying to embarrass me." Imprisoning her with his flinty gaze, his voice dropped ominously. "I'll not have it, Miss Fairingdale. I was kind enough to receive you today, and I have endured your endless letters, but this is the outside of enough."

The feathers tickled at the nape of her neck as she gazed mutinously up into his face. *He* had had enough! She was the one who had been obliged to make the long journey all the way from Manchester. "Then give me fifty thousand pounds and I shall go away."

"Miss Fairingdale, that is blackmail."

"Don't be ridiculous. You are rich. Everyone says so. You haven't a wife or any children to support. You would scarcely miss a few pounds. Besides," she added fairly, "I would repay it in time."

He stalked to the end of the balcony, then swung around and moved back toward her until the light streaming through the double doors formed a softening nimbus around him. When he spoke, though, his voice was rough and final. "I'll not give you a sou–and there's an end to it."

If he thought that was the end of it, he really did not know her, Arabella thought with cold defiance. Still, it accomplished little to stand here and shout at each other. She steadied herself with a calming breath, put her hands on either side of her on the cool, gritty balustrade, and tired for reason. "At least agree to go to Manchester." Once she got him there, she could make him see how bad it was.

"No."

"Then send your man of business to survey the books."

"I shall do so in good time." He stopped near her, but he was still too far in the shadows for her to see his face. "Naturally, I intend to look at the books eventually, but the mill is the least of the many properties I own."

"The mill may only earn a small profit each year, but certain things should be done because they are the right thing to do," she told him in a starched voice.

"You are exaggerating."

His dismissing tone only served to incense her more. "I am not. Furthermore, I intend to put myself in your path at every opportunity. I shall follow you into a dozen other card rooms and try to speak to you whenever I can. I shall also return to your house."

He moved a step closer and his voice tightened. "Are you trying to create a scandal?"

"Certainly not," Arabella said, with dignity. "That is the furthest thing from my mind. I fail to see how making you aware of your duties would create a scandal."

"I refer to your visits to my house."

"There will be no talk if I bring my companion. Scandals are caused by late night trysts, and unsuitable matches, and indiscreet love affairs. I am certain we shall not be involved in any of those."

"Not likely," he muttered. After a long silence, he snapped, "Very well, I shall send someone to the mill to investigate your concerns. Surely that will satisfy you."

Arabella nodded. A slow smile brushed across her face like a stirring wind after a long period of calm. She would prefer that he go himself, but this would do. She could be ready to travel to Manchester as early as Wednesday. It might, she admitted reluctantly, take longer for the marquess to arrange for someone to go on his behalf. In that event, she would have to be patient and wait.

Alas, patience was not her strength.

As Arabella watched, the marquess's angular features softened into the curves of a smile. For the first time she understood why women flocked to him. He looked very appealing in his expensive gray coat and with his hair curling slightly at the dark ends.

"Is anything wrong?" he asked.

Suddenly aware that she was watching him too closely, Arabella glanced away and said sensibly, "I am glad we have come to a solution. It just goes to prove that two people of intelligence can always sort out their problems."

"Or at least come to a compromise."

Arabella nodded. She did not tell him that she would not be satisfied with a compromise for long. Eventually the marquess must go to Manchester himself. For now, though, sending someone else would do. With a bright smile, Arabella allowed Lord Ridgeton to escort her back inside.

* * *

"Leave London in the midst of the Season! My dear, you cannot mean it." Lady Hector set her teacup on the table beside the blue settee, touched her fingers to her dark satin turban, and stared speechlessly at Arabella.

"I didn't come for the routs and soirees. I came to see Lord Ridgeton. Now that he has agreed to have someone inspect the mill, there is no reason for me to remain."

"No reason to remain?" she repeated incredulously. "What utter nonsense. Don't you enjoy the parties?"

Arabella looked about at a front parlor dense with thick blue draperies and gilt-encrusted furniture. The morning visitors had already appeared and departed; Lady Hector and Arabella were now alone.

"I enjoy the parties very much." Arabella ran her fingers down a kerseymere dress as green as the fields of England. The fabric had come from a gown Lady Hector no longer wore.

"You simply must stay." The older woman eyed Arabella shrewdly. "Men are beginning to notice you. I heard your name mentioned several times last night, and one of the callers this morning seemed particularly interested in you. If you remained, who knows what might happen?"

Arabella laughed. "Lady Hector, you know I am too long on the shelf to be considered for a wife." Or at least to be considered by the laughing, loving sort of man she would wish. She did not add that she would not want portly, middle-aged Mr. Hammonds even though he had complimented her on the pretty glow on her cheeks. Arabella knew it was the flush of triumph. She was still savoring last night's victory with the marquess.

"I still fail to see why you do not remain for the whole of the Season," Lady Hector insisted. "You will miss such fun and excitement. What amusements can there be for you in Kent? What do you do there?"

"I wrote all of Lady Baxter's correspondence before her death, and I had free run of her library. I taught drawing to a few of the village children. Well," Arabella amended truthfully, "I started out teaching drawing. But then Emily began to tell stories. Soon dozens of children appeared at our doorstep. I honestly do not know where they all came from. It was wondrous fun, though."

"It may have been," the countess said, without conviction, "but it could hardly occupy you all the time."

"Oh, I found dozens of ways to amuse myself. One summer I sewed together my old petticoats and Mr. Wilkes and I attached them to a large wicker basket to make our own air balloon. It did not fly, but Mr. Wilkes believes it will once we repair the wicker that was torn when it crashed."

"Small wonder it crashed," Lady Hector snipped. "The man is insane, my dear. He has worked in my stables the past few days building a machine that is supposed to run on steam or air or some such thing. It makes a dreadful amount of noise."

"It is a road locomotive."

"It sounds dangerous. I only hope he knows what he is about."

"Oh, indeed. Mr. Wilkes has been an inventor forever." Well, Arabella amended with silent honesty, now and again he had an accident or an idea lacking in sense. The coffin with windows and trapdoor was one such invention. He had worked night and day to perfect it. He had also worked to help Emily by stringing ropes with different knots throughout the house in Kent to lead her from one room to the other. Unfortunately the ropes had to be taken down when the scullery maid tripped and nearly fell into the cellar.

Arabella drew the talk from Mr. Wilkes and back to her departure. "I shall not go directly to Kent. I shall go to Manchester first."

"Manchester! How dreadful. There are no parties there. No culture at all."

Arabella laughed. "I am not going for the parties." She did feel an unexpected regret that she would not be able to spin about in a waltz just a time or two more. She had found it surprisingly pleasurable to be held captive in a man's arms while the music swelled and subsided. It was foolishness, of course, and she marked it down to never having had a Season.

"When will you leave?"

"I don't know yet. I must send a note to Lord Ridgeton, so we can discuss the day." Frowning down at the expensive Persian rug, she worked the pile back and forth with the tip of her kid slipper. She had not told the marquess she wished to go to Manchester with the man he intended to send, but surely Lord Ridgeton understood as much. Just to be safe, though, she had better tell him so.

"You are not going alone, are you?" the countess asked in a worried voice.

"No." Arabella rose amid a cascade of green kerseymere and walked past the carved marble fireplace to the row of windows glistening in the midday sun. "Lord Ridgeton is sending a man to examine the mill and I shall accompany him."

"You cannot travel in a closed carriage with a man all the way to Manchester!" The plume bobbed in outrage atop Lady Hector's head.

"I won't be alone. I shall have Emily."

The countess's frown deepened. "Arabella, Emily

is a lovely woman, but she is no more than two years older than you and she is blind."

"Not entirely blind. She can make out shapes if the light is good. She needs assistance to move about, but she is working very hard to overcome the problem. She helps me dress and is learning to do a good many things by touch. Emily is surprisingly adept at buttons."

"My dear," the countess said, with gentle concern. "You must realize a blind companion would hardly save your name from scandal."

"I daresay the furor of the scandal would depend on the age and appearance of the man Lord Ridgeton sends to Manchester," Arabella noted practically. "If he sends someone stout and ancient, my reputation would surely survive."

"What if Lord Ridgeton sends someone as handsome and virile as himself?" Lady Hector asked challengingly.

"People might talk, but it would be a nine days' wonder." People had talked after Mama's death when Arabella and her father had continued to move about the countryside. They had stayed at inns and with friends and Papa had taught school and worked on his inventions. Arabella had felt quite unfettered and happy. It was not until some of Mama's shocked friends plucked her away to go to Miss Landrum's boarding school that she realized how unconventional her life was.

Lady Hector shook her head, but an indulgent gleam showed in her eyes. "You're incorrigible, but I can scarcely scold you. I was much the same at your age."

Arabella was silent. Mama had told her about the dashing young man who had captured a younger Lady Hector's heart. He was a squire's son from an impoverished branch of the lofty Windlemere family. The young lovers had been set to elope to Gretna Green when Lady Hector's father intervened. A year later a subdued Lady Hector had married the earl and no one ever heard of the young man again. Did Lady Hector think about him still? she wondered.

That, Arabella decided, was being foolishly romantic. She had far more practical affairs to attend to. She must contact Lord Ridgeton and make her desire to go to Manchester known to him. Then she would visit Sir David, who was an expert on the subject of reform in the mills.

So far everything was moving along well. Arabella could not imagine any problems presenting themselves.

Clad only in the unmentionables he had worn to the rout last night, the marquess stood in his long, narrow dressing room and glared down at Harry. Lord Ridgeton's hair was still ruffled with sleep and his wide, bare chest showed the creases from the bedclothes. His valet, Charles, peeped curiously at Harry's darkening bruises and at the nasty cut tracing from his forehead to the edge of his eyebrow.

"Well, Harry, what have you to say for yourself?" Lord Ridgeton demanded. Only months separated the men in age, but the marquess sometimes felt like a father to the hapless Harry. Not that he hadn't been a scapegrace in his salad days, but even after his worst fights, he had never looked like this.

"There were three of 'em," Harry mumbled.

Charles gasped.

The marquess turned to his valet. "Go find something to put on Mr. Bartley's injuries."

"Yes, milord."

Lord Ridgeton waited for the door to close before

lifting an eyebrow and inquiring conversationally, "Harry, do you wish to be killed?"

"Of course not." He gingerly touched a purple bruise on his cheek and winced.

The marquess ran his fingers through the scattering of dark hair on his chest and stalked the length of the narrow red room. "Then why must you persist in playing at investigator?" He stopped, jammed his hands into his tight trousers, and glared at Harry.

"It's perfectly respectable. You know you cannot always depend on the Bow Street Runners to get your stolen silver back. That's when I am called in to assist. I'm well paid for my work," he added proudly.

"I'll wager you earn little more than twenty pounds, and you are most assuredly not in need of money."

"No, I don't need the blunt," Harry agreed readily. "I do it because it's exciting."

The excitement only seemed worthwhile for someone with better fists and quicker reflexes than Harry. The marquess himself might be suited for the work, but he had no interest in it. The war had dimmed his enthusiasm for suffering, particularly his own.

"You ought to understand a need for excitement," Harry added in wounded accents. "After all, you went off to fight when you didn't have to. It's not as if you were a younger brother forced to join the military."

"I daresay you won't believe this, Harry, but I fought out of loyalty to my country and not because I relished the romance of being blown to bits."

"Why won't you talk about it then? It must have been glorious." Harry's eyes lit with enthusiasm and he leaned forward eagerly for details.

"Only those who were not there think the campaigns with Wellington were glorious," Lord Ridgeton said wrily. Those who had not been there did not know about the unstaunched blood or the anguish of watching companions die. They didn't know about living in grit and filth. Those memories remained all too vivid for the marquess. He woke up many nights haunted by them. He wished he could put the nightmares behind him and lose himself in the mindless diversions of the London Season. So far he had not been able to.

"Being a hero makes it dashed easy to attract women, too. Not," Harry added mournfully, "that you suffer any trouble in that regard."

The marquess was not so modest as to deny his ability to charm women. The devil of it was that he was no longer interested in conquests. Serena Morris, a diamond of the first water and the reigning belle of the Season, had made it plain she would welcome his attentions. He had not even bothered to call on her. Nor had he taken a mistress since his return.

There were plenty of ladybirds to be had for the price of a few jewels and pretty gowns. He didn't even feel a flutter of interest.

The knock on the door jarred him out of his ruminations. "I don't wish to be disturbed," he barked.

"Have you a bottle of something strong?" Harry tugged at a cravat that was already wildly askew.

The marquess pulled a decanter of amber-colored liquid from a gold tray and handed a glass to Harry.

The knock sounded again.

"Blast." Lord Ridgeton jerked the door open and stared down at the servant who stood uneasily outside the door. "What is it?"

"Begging your pardon, milord, but this just came.

I would not have disturbed you, but it is marked urgent."

It was, indeed, and in the same bold, abrupt script Cedric had come to associate with Miss Fairingdale's letters. He took the envelope and closed the door.

"Urgent?" Harry asked curiously.

Lord Ridgeton ripped open the envelope and scanned the letter. "Accompanying my man north! Not bloody likely, girl," he muttered, and wadded the letter into an inelegant ball.

Harry sank into a chair with phoenix heads on the arms and gulped the last of the liquor. "Is there a problem, Cedric?"

"No, there is not a problem. I am sending someone to Manchester to investigate Miss Fairingdale's claims of problems—groundless, I don't doubt—and she wants to journey with the man. Such empty-headed idiocy."

"Who is going?" Harry asked as the marquess circled the length of the narrow red room like a caged lion.

He shrugged. "One of my groomsmen perhaps. Or the coachman. He has family near there and would be glad of the opportunity to visit." It would be inconvenient to be without a servant during the Season, but there appeared to be no help for it.

"You are sending someone to *investigate* and you think just anyone can manage? A groomsman?" Harry asked in outraged accents. "Why not send someone skilled in these matters? Why not send me?"

The marquess stopped pacing. "God's teeth, Harry. You're black and blue from last night's 'investigation.' How skilled can you be?" He regretted the words as soon as they were out. Harry was not the most brilliant man in the world, but he was sincere and his feelings were easily hurt. Even now a crestfallen expression was spreading over his florid, boyish face.

"I think I'm skilled enough," he mumbled. "Everyone makes a mistake now and again."

"Of course they do," he agreed. "I didn't mean to disparage you. Here, have some more port." The marquess splashed liquor into Harry's upraised glass and pondered the idea. Manchester would certainly be safe. In fact, it might be the very place to send Harry to get him away from the back alleys of London, where he took more than his share of pummelings. It would make Harry's mama endlessly happy to have her son removed from the path of harm.

"Would Miss Fairingdale accompany me?"

"No," Lord Ridgeton said, with finality.

"Oh," he said flatly. "I rather like her. She has a pretty smile. Little dimples, and flashing blue eyes, and nice, even teeth."

Arabella Fairingdale's delicate features hid an iron will. "She is not going anywhere. She has done enough damage as it is. Pity she didn't marry some man who would rein her in." Although finding such a man would not be easy with a woman like her. "At any rate, I think it would be an excellent idea for you to go to Manchester."

Harry snapped to attention. "Knew you'd come round, Cedric. What am I to do there?"

Do? It was a fool's errand, so there was really little to do. "Go to the mill, look about a bit, and come back and report what you saw."

Harry frowned and rubbed at a bruise. "It doesn't sound very exciting."

"If you'd like to acquire a few more scars, I'm sure that can be arranged," the marquess said drily. "Are you an investigator or not?"

"Most assuredly." He emphasized it with a firm nod.

"Good. It's settled."

"I shall leave tonight, as soon as darkness falls."

"Why the devil wait until it is dark?"

"An investigator always works at night," Harry said, with solemn authority.

"Ahh." It was difficult to be cross with someone as naive and good-natured as Harry.

Lord Ridgeton would wait a day or two and then explain to Arabella that he had dispatched someone north. She would not be pleased, but there would be little she could do at that point. He was being generous to send someone to Manchester at all; he owed her nothing beyond that.

Somehow, though, he did not believe she would see matters that way.

Arabella perched on the edge of a wooden chair, unable to sit back due to the stack of books behind her. The table was also piled high with tomes, as was the floor around her.

Sir David pulled yet another volume from an upper shelf. "Ah, here is *New Views of Society*. You should read this as well."

Arabella had come to see Sir David because he was a friend of Robert Owen's; both men believed passionately in bettering the conditions of factory workers. She was eager to begin work in that direction, but she had not expected to feel so overwhelmed. She looked doubtfully at the teetering stack of books. "I don't know when I shall have time to read all this."

"You must, child, and then read them again. Our future is at stake here." Sir David regarded her from behind his crowded desk. Arabella thought he looked very wise with his white tufts of hair, full beard, and bushy mustache. He wore a black garb and possessed the kindly appearance of a vicar. When he talked, though, fire flashed in his eyes.

"You know, of course, about the distress that has followed the peace. It is going to get worse. The workers must have some relief." He spread his hands in an impassioned gesture and continued, "It is not only the peace that has brought about unemployment. Spread of machinery has hurt workers, too. The war caused an increase in machinery, but now that it is over we are left with a productive power that has the effect of a twentyfold increase in population." He rummaged on the desk for another book, found it, and held it aloft. "Read this, it will help explain."

Arabella didn't think she could even carry all these books to the door. She appreciated his fervor, but she needed to limit the scope or she would spend the rest of her life reading and never accomplish anything. "You see, Sir David, I only own a single mill. I wish to start there to improve the lot of the workers."

He looked at her a long, considering moment, then nodded in rueful apology. "I forget myself. When good people come to me, I try to tell them everything all at once." He smiled and searched vaguely about on the crowded desk. "You have seen the mill?"

"Yes."

"Does it have spinning frames and powerlooms?"

"I do not know, but it has a great deal of fast and dangerous equipment. Those who work there daily risk losing fingers and arms." She had shivered at the sight of the quick machinery and the tiny fingers of the children who tended it.

"Does it have metal columns and joists for fireproofing?" he asked.

Arabella felt woefully ignorant. "I cannot say."

His smile softened kindly. "It is all right. I shall draw up a list of all the things that might need to be considered for improvement."

Arabella nodded in relief. "Good." She wanted to sound knowledgeable and efficient when she talked again with the marquess. She also wanted to let him know she had spoken with a man who was well versed in the matter. Lord Ridgeton might be able to dismiss her, but he could not dismiss someone as learned as Sir David.

The older man paused in the act of reaching for a sheet of paper. "I believe you said you had a partner. Does he agree with what you mean to do?"

Arabella hesitated only an instant. "Not yet, perhaps, but he will."

"Then you have found a rare person indeed."

"Lord Ridgeton is a good man." Perhaps he was not a *wonderful* man, but he had agreed to send someone to Manchester.

"Lord Ridgeton of Salisbury?" At her nod, Sir David cleared his throat and pulled at a tuft of hair on his right side. "I was not given to understand that he was a man of great social conscience."

"He may not be yet," she leaned forward to confide, "I am going to make him such a man."

The old man's laughter was low and rich. "Will you indeed?"

"Yes. I see him as a rough stone that only needs a bit of polishing."

Sir David threw back his head and bellowed with laughter. "You may be able to accomplish it, my dear. You certainly don't lack determination." Still grinning, he ran his fingers through the thicket of his beard. "Very well, then. Let me see. You must begin by making certain that housing is provided at a decent rent. A store run by the mill would help the employees buy food and clothing. Gardens for social recreation would be nice but not essential to begin with. Be sure to read about Mr. Owen's work at New Lanark Mills."

Arabella listened attentively, warmed by the knowledge she and the marquess were going to improve the lot of their workers.

Chapter 3

LORD RIDGETON sat astride his white stallion Winter and doffed his hat toward Lady Sefton's carriage. Up ahead, he noticed the odd vehicle with large wheels in front and small ones in back. The closed carriage bounced along amid the parade of fashionable curricles and satin-lined barouches. The same odd man the marquess had seen before sat bent over the reins. The man was dressed in blue brocade and wore a tricorn hat. The unusual spectacle was drawing a number of stares.

"Who in the devil is that?" Lord Peterby asked from atop his spirited bay.

"Haven't the least notion." That was not entirely true. The marquess had a niggling suspicion he did know—but he hoped he was wrong.

As they drew nearer, a trim arm appeared through the window and a face followed it. Blond curls flirted at the sides of a cream-colored bonnet. He had to admit that Arabella Fairingdale made a charming picture as she waved to him. That did not change the fact he was thoroughly dismayed to see her.

The earl looked at him with sharp interest. "The lady knows you."

"A passing acquaintance." Blast. He could not turn back in this throng. It was the fashionable hour on Rotten Row; to attempt to ride in the opposite direction would be to court death. The marquess had no choice but to go forward, toward her.

A few moments later he drew alongside the coach. It was a monstrosity, but Arabella looked surprisingly pretty framed in the window. Her cheeks were the color of pink petals and her fluffy blond curls made a delicate lacing around her face. She smiled directly at him and an answering smile pried his mouth upward.

"I am so pleased to see you, Lord Ridgeton."

He ignored Lord Peterby's stare. "It is my pleasure entirely to see you, Miss Fairingdale."

"Did you receive my note?" Her words were polite—but her eyes glinted a rather steely blue.

"Yes. I received it yesterday."

"I am persuaded I shall hear from you soon?"

"You may depend on it." Harry had already left town, so it was too late for her to accompany him northward. Lord Ridgeton would have to tell her, but not here and not now—especially not when she looked as if she wanted to trust him but hesitated to do so. He had seen that doubt before on women's faces but had always charmed it away with murmured endearments and vague promises. He did not think Miss Fairingdale would be fobbed off so easily. Besides, his dealings with other women had been for pleasure; his association with her was business only.

Just then the jam ahead loosened and horses and curricles and landaus began to jostle again. She gave a final wave with a gloved hand before disappearing into the carriage.

Beside him, Lord Peterby drawled, "Would you like to tell me who that was, Cedric?"

"Miss Fairingdale," he said tersely, and offered no further explanation.

"She isn't in your usual way. You've always preferred actresses with thick, dark hair. And women who own stylish barouches. Harriet Wilson would have never stepped foot in that traveling menace."

"Miss Fairingdale is not a cyprian. She is a guest of Lady Hector's."

Lord Peterby glanced back over his shoulder. "She is clearly not encumbered with a fortune." His voice thickened suggestively. "Still, she seems full of life and she has a fetching face. I should like to know her better. Do you expect she will be at the Millers' soiree tonight?"

The marquess jerked at the reins. He might not approve of Miss Fairingdale, but he did not wish to see her become embroiled with a rake like Peterby. "I do not know what her plans for the evening might be."

"I expect Lady Hector will go to the Millers' party," Lord Peterby mused aloud. "The two women are good friends. In that event, Lady Hector's guest, Miss Fairingdale, is bound to go, too. I believe I shall make an appearance there."

He stiffened at the notion of the earl luring Arabella into a dark garden to steal kisses. Or worse.

"Miss Fairingdale is an unprotected lady. Since she came to London to see me, I would consider it my duty to protect her if the need arose." The chit was putting him in more awkward positions than he would have thought possible. Still, she had no other male to protect her, so he was obliged to behave as a gentleman.

Lord Peterby passed a slow, measuring look over him before noting cynically: "Rather like a fox guarding the chickens to have a saucy little baggage like that under *your* protection, isn't it, Cedric?"

"I do not seduce ladies!" he snapped, and reined in his horse when the crowd slowed again.

Peterby chuckled. "Doing it a bit brown for one who has taken his pleasures in some rather exalted bedchambers. Before you fought with Wellington, you were known to have sampled a few feminine wares."

The marquess's mouth folded into a guilty smile. "I may have sown some wild oats during my salad days, but I never compromised a lady of Quality." He had never had to. There had been enough pretty widows and experienced courtesans to satisfy his hunger.

Peterby shrugged. "Let's not quarrel over women. What say we go to Tattersall's to examine the new horseflesh?"

"I think not today."

"That's what you said last week. What the devil is wrong with you, Cedric? When I proposed a midnight picnic with some actresses, you declined that, too. Dammit, you've been back in London over two months. You ought to enjoy yourself."

The marquess did not argue. He knew he was not himself, but any day things would return to normal. His interest in racing and women would revive. He would become entranced by some vixen and begin deriving pleasure from the social whirl. Any day it was bound to happen.

But as he entered his chambers after returning home, he knew he had not the least interest in attending the Millers' soiree. He would only be bored doing the pretty to women who did not interest him. He would not even find diversion in the gaming room.

Charles was laying out clothes for the evening, lovingly smoothing the cravat, when Lord Ridgeton stalked into the dressing room and announced: "I'm not going to the party tonight. Pack a few clothes. I mean to go see Layton."

The horrified valet let the cravat slip from his fingers. "You don't intend to leave today?"

"Yes." His arrival would be unannounced and unexpected, but he thought Layton would be glad to see him. It was only two hours of hard riding, and he felt a restlessness that the ride might cure. Certainly it would lift Layton's spirits to see an old friend. The man must be sunk in depression.

The ride took closer to three hours, but Lord Ridgeton was feeling exhilarated when he arrived shortly after nightfall. A servant showed him into a small back room where Layton sat reading a book. The crippled man laid it aside and blinked at the marquess.

"Ridgeton? What the devil are you doing here?"

"Is that any way to greet a fellow soldier? I've come all the way from London to visit you."

"Are you mad? Why would you leave London during the height of the Season to visit a man missing an eye and half a leg?"

The marquess crossed the room in easy strides. Layton's black eye patch was gone; his missing eye seemed bent into a perpetual wink that made his broad face look almost mischievous. Layton looked relaxed; he did not even throw a cover over the stump of leg stuck out in front of him on a footrest. "I was bored with London."

The crippled man nodded. "After the battles we saw together, I expect I would be bored even if I were whole." He motioned toward a chair nearby. "Sit and talk to me. You can stay a day or two, can't you?"

"Yes. I have nothing pressing awaiting me in London."

"Splendid. I've longed for someone of intelligence to happen by. The chess board is already set up."

Lord Ridgeton settled into a cool leather chair. It

felt good to be with someone who knew about the battles and who didn't beg to hear glorious descriptions of them. He and Layton could talk or not and the silences would be just as comfortable as their most heated exchanges.

"You can ride with me tomorrow to inspect the estate," his host said.

"You ride?" he asked in amazement.

"Of course. I only lost part of a leg and an eye, Cedric. I can still get about and see well enough to terrorize the servants. I've even managed to persuade a young lady to have me."

"You mean you are to wed?"

Layton laughed. "Don't sound so astonished. Did you think I was sitting here withering away and never leaving the house?"

That was precisely what he had thought, but he did not say so. Instead he sat silently and marveled at the fact Layton seemed perfectly content with the world. Why, then, couldn't he—a whole man—find such contentment?

The day following Arabella's encounter with Lord Ridgeton in the Park, she waited for word from him. None came. She was disappointed but distracted herself by reading the books Sir David had lent her. Sometimes the reading was tedious, but she gleaned a great deal of information to present to Lord Ridgeton. Still, she occasionally went to the window to look out and wonder where he was.

By Thursday Arabella had grown more restless; it was all she could do to concentrate on sewing trim on a gown she was making over for a small rout. By Friday she was impatient.

Saturday she was just plain angry.

The wretch had been full of smiles and charm when they had met on Rotten Row, yet he had not called on her as he had promised. Well, she was not some shrinking violet who would endure his silence forever. She would go to his house and demand an explanation. Today was as good a day as any.

With that in mind, Arabella called Emily to help her dress in a sea green gown. Emily was struggling to fasten the buttons up the back when a knock sounded.

Lady Hector opened the door and smiled. "Ah, good. I see you are dressing. I was afraid you had forgotten that my salon meets today."

She bit her lip guiltily. Oh dear, was that today? The countess had mentioned her salon, but it had sounded so dull that Arabella had promptly put it from her mind.

"I am so glad you will join us. It is not intellectual or political like Lady Holland's salon," Lady Hector added half apologetically. "It is only a gathering of friends to exchange news. The women are all above fifty, but I do not think you will be bored."

"Of course not." Arabella offered her sunniest smile. "I look forward to joining you."

After the door closed behind Lady Hector, Emily asked, "Are you disappointed that you will not be able to see His Lordship today?"

"Yes. I can go after the guests leave if it is not too late." Arabella set her jaw angrily. "I should have demanded an answer when I met the cad in the Park. Imagine telling me he would send me word and never doing so. This may be how he deals with *other* women, but he shall not deal with *me* in this manner."

"You said yourself you have not seen him at any of the events you have attended. Perhaps he is ill."

She was not so easily mollified.

"He could still have sent a note."

"It does seem so," Emily agreed mildly. "Perhaps

you will see him at the rout tonight. Here, let me brush your hair."

An hour later, Arabella sat on a lacquered chair in the front parlor listening to the older women talk about sons and daughters and grandchildren. With a smile fixed on her face, she tried to maintain a look of polite interest—while she silently fumed about Lord Ridgeton.

During a lull in the conversation, silver-haired Lady Ashton turned to Arabella. "Is it true you inherited a mill?"

"Yes."

"How extraordinary," the elderly woman said.

"Yes, I intend to make many improvements. I shall go to Manchester soon to begin making decisions."

Lady Ashton stared in astonishment. "Surely *you* will not be *directly* involved. My child, such tasks should be left to men."

"Only if they are good and responsible men." Papa had been good—but he had not been responsible. So far Lord Ridgeton was not showing himself to be either.

Oh, Arabella did not doubt he would eventually send someone to look at the books, but he would not act with any unnecessary speed. She had asked to see the books when she was in Manchester and the overseer, a thoroughly disagreeable man named Mr. Daley, had grudgingly presented them to her. Arabella had spent hours perusing the jumble of figures and rows of numbers before admitting someone with business skill needed to examine the books.

Arabella's wandering attention was drawn back into the discussion when one of the women remarked, "I understand Harry Bartley left on another of his foolish errands. He went somewhere to the north, I believe."

Mrs. Plenham sighed theatrically. "Poor man. His dear mother worries so about him. If it were not that she and Lady Ridgeton are particular friends and Lord Ridgeton looks after Harry, I fear Harry would come to grave harm."

Lady Ashton lowered her voice. "Indeed he would. Have you heard about the night Lord Ridgeton was obliged to go to some dreadful part of the rookery to rescue Harry? It's said Lord Ridgeton fought two men with his bare hands."

"I heard it was three men, Emma."

Lady Ashton stiffened at having her facts questioned. "At any rate, Lord Ridgeton has been a good friend to Harry Bartley."

Pity he was not proving such a friend to his employees, Arabella thought uncharitably. Where had the man been these last days? His name had now and again arisen in conversation at routs, but no one knew where he was. Arabella could not credit that he was going to so much trouble to avoid her.

The conversation moved on to a discussion of flattering colors for women with gray hair. Arabella's interest was again fading when Lady Ashton said, "I have heard Lord Seagraves has returned from the Colonies and is in London."

Arabella tapped her fingers on the side of the lacquered chair and waited impatiently to hear more. Lord Seagraves was Lady Baxter's nephew and the man who had inherited the estate where Arabella lived. Her future was in his hands.

"I wonder if he is as wild as his father. The elder Lord Seagraves was killed in a duel, you know." Lady Ashton lowered her voice and continued, "Over a very disreputable woman."

"I am certain Lord Seagraves is a fine young

man," Lady Hector said stoutly. "I have heard nothing but good things concerning him."

Arabella hoped the countess was right. She would be in a very awkward situation if she were forced to leave the estate and find another place to live. Where else could Mr. Wilkes stay up late into the night laboring over his inventions in the barn? Where else could Emily learn to overcome her blindness except in familiar surroundings? Where else could Arabella afford to live?

"Dear me, look at the time." Lady Ashton pushed herself to her feet. "I must go in order to have time to stop at the lending library on the way home."

The rest of the women departed shortly afterward in a fluttering of shawls and kisses.

When the last one was gone, Arabella looked at the clock on the mantel and saw with regret it was too late to call on the marquess today.

There was nothing to be done but wait until tomorrow. Meanwhile the Westfields' ball was tonight. She had not seen Lord Ridgeton at any other party this past week, but everyone of any consequence at all would attend tonight's ball. Surely he would be there.

With that in mind, Arabella went upstairs to begin preparations for the evening. Three hours later she sat in front of the mirror while Emily arranged her hair. Arabella sometimes guided Emily's hands, and the two of them brushed and curled until Arabella's blond hair was nestled gleaming and tamed around her face. Taking great care not to disturb those burnished curls, Arabella stepped into a maroon gown with silver piping around the low, square neck and allowed Emily to fasten the tiny buttons up the back.

As Emily worked, Arabella studied herself in the cheval glass. The dark dress made her eyes look large and darker blue. The gown also made her face appear paler, accenting the soft color on her cheekbones. She was not vain, but gentlemen had begun to notice her, and she took a feminine appreciation of the fact she could still, at five-and-twenty, draw attention.

"Mr. Wilkes is working on another invention for me," Emily announced.

Arabella bit her lip. "Oh, dear. What is it?"

"A stick with a wheel that I can roll down the sidewalk in front of me. He thinks it will knock anything in my path aside. He is working on a bell to ring if someone does not get out of my way quickly enough."

Laughing, Arabella shook her head and sent the curls bobbing. "It will be good to be back at the Baxter estate where he can work without worrying Lady Hector." She only hoped the new master had no objections to Mr. Wilkes's inventions.

"I am done." Emily stepped back. "Does it look good?"

"Yes. I shall put the rich little misses to shame," she said wickedly.

Emily smiled.

Arabella picked up her pelisse and walked out the door and down the stairs. Lady Hector was waiting for her in the large foyer.

"How pretty you look, Arabella. You shall catch the eye of every man there."

Arabella was interested in only one man—and that was only because she wished to demand an accounting from him. All the way to the Westfield mansion, she nursed her anger over his callous disregard for her. Did he think he could fob her off with empty promises? He would soon learn he could not.

The grand Westfield house was ablaze with

lights. Arabella entered with a smile in place and a militant gleam in her eye as she gazed about the crowd. It was not long before she spied Lord Ridgeton. He was leaning forward to whisper into the ear of a pretty redhead. Arabella shot an icy stare across the room at him.

He must have felt the weight of her glare, for he raised his head and looked across the room toward her. Their eyes met and he inclined his head politely, crossed to her, and bowed over her hand. "How charming to see you, Miss Fairingdale."

She sank a hard look into him. How dare he be so calm and guiltless? "I have been most anxious to see you, milord," she said tartly, and lifted her chin until the small pointed end of it was aimed at him. "I am packed and ready to leave whenever you say."

Elderly duchess Lady Wells, who was seated on a flaming red settee nearby, raised scandalized eyebrows.

Ignoring her, Arabella continued. "It *will* be this week when we go, won't it? I am too impatient to wait longer."

Did Lady Wells gasp? Arabella didn't care. She fought to remain cordial to Lord Ridgeton. He might look like a gentleman in his claret-colored coat and pearl gray unmentionables, but he had behaved like a scoundrel.

Lord Ridgeton glanced at the duchess and pitched his voice louder for her benefit. "Your impatience for the welfare of the workers is a credit to you, Miss Fairingdale."

"*You* have certainly not been concerned about them. Or about me. You promised you would send word about the trip to Manchester, yet I have heard nothing." She tightened her grip on the ivory handle of her fan and glared at him.

He took her arm and guided her toward the door.

"Where are we going?"

"Outside. We can scarcely stand on the floor and shout at each other."

"Pray why not?" she asked acidly. "Would that be as rude as avoiding me these past days? I am ready to go to Manchester. When will your man leave?"

Lady Wells leaned closer so as not to miss a word.

He pulled her out onto the balcony. "He has already left."

For a long, disbelieving moment, Arabella blinked up into Lord Ridgeton's shrouded brown eyes and aristocratically notched face. Had she heard him right? One look at his stone-cold face convinced her that she had. "How could you?" she finally sputtered.

He had the grace to look guilty before lifting his shoulders defiantly. His expression hardened. "It was out of the question for an unmarried woman to make such a journey with a man. I had your reputation to consider."

"You know perfectly well I have a companion."

"Well, it is done—and arguing will not change matters."

Arabella yanked her arm from his grip and grasped the fan even tighter. "I think you're horrid." The words were mild compared to the torrent of anger she wanted to unleash on him, but it would serve no purpose to do so. She whirled to leave . . . but he caught her arm again. "Let me go!"

"Arabella, don't shout. You'll raise the house."

"I don't care."

"I do. We left the room together." He held fast to her wrist as he continued, "If you storm back inside alone, people will think I attempted something improper."

"You may not have made improper advances, but you betrayed me all the same," she said in scalding accents.

He shook his head wearily. "I know you think I betrayed you, but I acted for the best. I am sorry I did not come to see you earlier, but I left town for a short time."

"You could have sent a message."

"Look, I sent someone to Manchester," he said sharply. "Surely that satisfies you."

He let go of her; she rubbed at her wrist and stared at him resentfully. "No, it doesn't satisfy me, but since you have seen fit to ignore my wishes, you might as well tell me who you sent and when you expect to hear something."

"His name is Harry Bartley. He is a detective."

"Harry Bartley! Why would you send someone as corkbrained as he? Well, you must send someone else immediately."

"Miss Fairingdale—"

She tossed back her head so sharply the pins fell and her hair danced loose. "You were never serious about this. You chose someone you knew would not do a proper job. I was foolish to trust you. I should have called at your house every day. I should have laid siege to you and made you miserable until you acted as a gentleman."

"No one has ever made me do anything I didn't wish to do," he informed her acidly.

"Stubbornness is never appealing, milord."

"Touché, Miss Fairingdale."

She shot him a blistering look.

It was evidently not blistering enough because amusement grew and flickered in the brown orbs of his eyes. His voice softened. "I know you don't believe me, but I am not trying to thwart you. I have gone out of my way to accommodate you and to protect you."

Protect her? What a ridiculous thing to say. "There's nothing to protect me from, Lord Ridgeton. I have been on my own long enough to take care of myself. If you refer to protecting me from traveling with a man, I know how to conduct myself."

During the long pause that followed that announcement, his gaze slid over her maroon gown, across the twin half-moons of bosom showing above the silver piping, and ended at her face. "I see. So if a gentleman held you too closely in the dance, you would simply slide away?"

"Of course."

"If he lured you into a dark garden and tried to kiss you, you would rap him on the wrist with your fan?"

"Yes."

He nodded as if absorbing her words, yet she noticed he moved a step closer.

They stood within touching distance, and suddenly Arabella's flush was not entirely from anger. She smelled the tobacco on him and saw the broad, near shape of his shoulders. It was no longer simply anger crackling in the air around them. Another emotion had been added . . . and Arabella did not want to consider what it was.

She did know, though, that the marquess seemed dangerous in an entirely new way.

Chapter 4

THE MOON disappeared behind a cloud and Arabella stood cloaked in darkness. She knew when Lord Ridgeton took another step toward her because she felt his breath blow through her hair. A moment later, strong arms touched her shoulders and something brushed her cheek. It might have been the kiss of the breeze or it might have been the back of the earl's hand caressing her gently. The gesture was too tender to warrant wrenching herself away. In fact, the touch made her catch her breath and wait in stillness to see what would follow.

"I—"

"Shhh."

Suddenly her mouth was caught in a soft, inviting kiss. The pressure of his lips ought not to have made her limbs turn sodden or her heartbeat flutter. She could have wrenched away, but the moment was so quietly romantic and his embrace so full of promise that she did not. Instead she stood full of wonder while his mouth roved atop hers, pressing harder and more urgently and rotating with gentle persuasion.

He pulled her closer against him and his mouth moved with greater urgency. Odd that the touch of a pair of lips could resonate throughout her body, making her fingertips tingle and causing a warm ball in her stomach to unravel and expand. Heat flowed down her arms and legs.

How was it possible to feel such fluttering yearnings when she did not trust him? How could his big hands splayed across her back make her feel secure when she was not even sure she liked him? Yet beneath logic ran the pure sensation of feeling, and Arabella very much liked the way her body felt in his embrace.

The kiss ended as quickly as it had begun, leaving her breathless and regretful that he had not lingered longer.

The moon was still a prisoner to the clouds when the marquess stepped away.

"Are you certain you can control every situation with men, Arabella?"

She had not given him leave to call her by her maiden name, but she was scarcely in a position to protest after having just enjoyed his kiss. The sound of his voice brought reality back to her. Why had she let him kiss her? The soft scent of the flowers around them and the moonlight had interfered with her logic, but she was sane again now.

"We have been in the garden long enough," she said crisply. "People will begin to wonder." If he noticed that she left his question unanswered, he did not say so. He took her arm and escorted her inside without another word.

At the doorway, Arabella scanned the room for the countess. When she saw her across the room, Arabella pulled away from the marquess and started toward Lady Hector. Arabella hoped the red spots on her cheeks did not look too alarming or her eyes too bright.

It was bad enough that she had been foolish enough to kiss the earl. It was worse that her pulse still hummed.

"My dear, I have been looking for you," the countess called to her. She turned to indicate the man standing beside her. "This is Lord Seagraves."

Arabella had not even noticed the man who was the new master of Baxter House. Now she surveyed him quickly. He was tall and his skin was burned a soft brown. His face was long and angular, and even the kindest soul could not call him handsome. He bowed low over her hand.

Arabella smiled prettily, anxious to make a good impression. It was hard to concentrate on him, though, when her thoughts were tangled like a kitten in string over the scene that had taken place in the garden.

"I have asked Lady Hector's permission to call on you tomorrow to discuss the tenant house," he said.

She swallowed heavily. Was she to be evicted?

He smiled and the homely face took on a gentler appearance. "Do not be alarmed. You may stay there as long as you wish, Miss Fairingdale. In fact, I would be infinitely grateful if you would remain."

"I appreciate your generosity." Her words seemed inadequate to convey her gratitude. She had not realized how worried she had been until now.

Had it not been for her confrontation with Lord Ridgeton, Arabella might have left the party feeling cheerful. As it was, she lay in her bed that night annoyed that the marquess had sent Harry Bartley to Manchester and wholly dissatisfied with herself for letting the marquess kiss her.

Yes, she had felt pleasure in his arms, but she would do well to remember he was practiced at seduction. The power of his kiss testified to his expertise. From now on, she would be on her guard against him.

* * *

Lord Ridgeton awoke the next day and lay in the big four-poster bed staring up at the canopy and debating whether he owed Arabella an apology for stealing a kiss. As he absently scratched his bare chest, he considered that she had not objected. In point of fact, she had seemed to enjoy the kiss almost as thoroughly as he.

She was not skilled, but she had seemed most willing to learn.

He was not in the habit of kissing ladies in gardens unless he had further designs on them. He had, of course, no further designs on Arabella Fairingdale. She had simply looked enticing in the moonlight with her eyes sparkling up at him. She had looked too beguiling not to embrace.

Tossing back the cover, he sat on the edge of the bed. His reaction to Arabella surely signaled a recovery from the malaise that had gripped him since his return from the Continent. If he could feel an interest in her, it was only a matter of time before he became attracted to one of the many comely chits being presented this Season. Certainly it could not be long before some beautiful, skilled cyprian caught his attention and he took her for a mistress.

Satisfied by the knowledge he was recovering, Lord Ridgeton called his valet and dressed for the day.

After a brief meeting with the steward from one of his lesser estates, he scanned the invitations and notes that had arrived for the day. There were soirees and card parties in abundance and he gave only cursory glances to those invitations. It was the note from his grandmother that caught his eye. "I shall expect you for tea tomorrow," she informed him.

He grinned. He could see the dainty little tyrant bent over her correspondence. She might be too frail to attend the events of the Season, but she still entertained callers and she still expected immediate responses when she summoned someone.

And he had definitely been summoned, he reflected as he left for his club. His visits with her were always interesting. She could be charming or dogmatic by turns, but she was never boring. He would find out tomorrow what she wished to say to him.

Half an hour later, he was seated in White's most comfortable chair reading the *Times* when a servant approached.

"A message for you, milord," he said deferentially.

Lord Ridgeton took the envelope, tore it open, and read the galloping script and scratched-out words:

Encountered a slight difficulty. Am in jail. Please see to my release. Yours, etc. Harry Bartley.

Groaning, the marquess sank back in the chair. He should have known better than to send Harry anywhere. Manchester had seemed so safe that he had thought no one could fall into a scrape there. What the devil had the fool done to get himself tossed in jail? He snapped the *Times* closed with such fierce irritation the pages tore.

Lord Peterby roused himself from a half slumber in the chair beside him. "Something amiss, Cedric?"

"Harry's got himself in a coil."

Peterby grinned. "That's to be expected, isn't it?"

"I daresay it is. Too bad I didn't possess such wisdom two weeks ago when I sent the shatterbrained fool off to Manchester. I should have sent someone to watch him."

The earl idly buffed his fingernails against his jacket. "What do you intend to do now?"

"Do? I shall have to get him out." Half to himself, he added, "And I shall have to inform Miss Fairingdale of this turn of events." That thought was almost as troublesome as having to arrange for Harry's release. He did not relish another dramatic scene with her.

Lord Peterby's expression turned cheerfully lecherous. "I would be happy to see Miss Fairingdale in your stead. I don't care that she rides about in that eccentric carriage or that she is no longer a schoolroom miss. She has a pretty countenance and the most fetching laugh I have heard in all the parlors of London." He paused before adding, "She's the only woman I know who actually hurts my knuckles when she raps them with her fan."

Lord Ridgeton regarded him darkly. "What did you do to give her cause to hit your knuckles?"

"I merely made an innocent suggestion." Peterby winked.

"You have not been innocent since you turned sixteen." In a sterner voice, the marquess warned, "You will recall that Miss Fairingdale is a proper young lady."

"Lud, Cedric. I can scarcely be blamed for noticing the chit. Half the men in London have."

Yes, they had. Lord Ridgeton had heard Arabella's name on men's lips everywhere, but no man had come forward to seriously court her. She might be fetching and lovely, but she was without a dowry and past the first blush of youth. It was possible that someone of the lesser ton would marry her, but equally possible someone like Peterby would lay less virtuous plans regarding her.

Arabella had said she could take care of herself, but that, of course, was foolishness. She was a mere slip of a woman and no physical match for the likes of Peterby or any other man.

The marquess thought of Arabella Fairingdale

tilting her face up toward him on the moonlit balcony. If she looked at other men with those magnificent blue eyes the way she looked at him, she could indeed be courting danger. It was not only Lord Peterby she had to fear, it was the whole damned crop of rakes.

"*You* are not interested in her, are you?"

"Of course not," the marquess said brusquely.

"Good thing. Although your mama is so anxious to see you wed, she might even accept Miss Fairingdale. But it is better to court Serena Morris if you mean to get shackled."

"You seem to be sending me into parson's trap with a certain amount of cheer," he noted drily.

"Maybe it would make you happy," Peterby said, with uncharacteristic philosophy. "Nothing else has since you got back from the Continent."

No, nothing had made him happy, he privately admitted.

It was time, Lord Ridgeton decided, to press himself into action. He clapped a hand on Peterby's shoulder. "You have the right of it. I have been behaving like an old man. Tonight you and I shall visit the tables, find a wild cockfight somewhere, and drink ourselves astonishingly happy."

"Actresses?" Peterby suggested wickedly.

"Of course! Ones with thick, dark hair. I don't want a blonde."

"Splendid. We must do the pretty first at the Manderbys' ball, but we can leave early."

On the way out of the club, it occurred to the marquess that Harry was still imprisoned in a cell in Manchester and that something must be done about that.

He would make a decision later. Right now, he felt a reckless determination to enjoy himself.

* * *

Arabella spent the day of the Manderbys' ball mending a torn gown and receiving visitors with Lady Hector. Afterward she visited Sir David again and spent a time reviewing her list of improvements with him. He made suggestions and nodded approval—and gave her more books to read.

Upon her return home, she and Emily went for a stroll and Emily practiced with Mr. Wilkes's new walking stick with its wheel and bell. The device caused a small dog a great deal of consternation. The dog growled and lunged at the stick until the dog's owner picked it up and carried it away and Arabella and Emily started slowly homeward.

Emily looked tired and anxious.

"Don't worry. I am persuaded most dogs will not be so unchivalrous," Arabella said.

"I feel foolish."

"Maybe the stick can accidentally be left behind when we leave London," Arabella suggested.

Emily sighed. "I daresay Mr. Wilkes would only build another one."

"He will be distracted with some other invention by then. Besides, you can tell him you are perfectly fine without the stick. It will be nothing less than the truth."

"I am doing well," Emily agreed, with pardonable pride. "Oh, I am still self-conscious about spilling food on myself, so I endeavor to eat alone, but for the most part I am becoming more adept at handling my blindness."

"You are," Arabella agreed. "Once we settle back into the house on Baxter estate where everything is familiar, you will improve even more." She thought again of her relief that Lord Seagraves would allow them to remain on the estate.

"Yes." Emily tucked the stick up under her arm

and put out a hand to follow a brick wall down the street. "How was your meeting with Sir David?"

"Interesting. He told me about cotton technology spreading from Yorkshire worsteds to linens and wools. Most of the time, though, he talked about the dreary lives of the workers."

"It must be sad for them."

"It is. Many work fourteen-hour days." Arabella had seen the small, airless rooms and the pale children and women toiling there all day long. It had hurt her to think they were working in such wretched conditions in a mill that she owned. Lord Ridgeton might choose to believe a man was better able to manage the mill, but men did not always have compassion. "Once Mr. Bartley returns from Manchester, I hope his descriptions will jolt Lord Ridgeton into awareness."

"It sounds as if the marquess's money would go a long way toward solving problems."

"It would." Arabella did not desire money for herself. She had learned to live simply. Still, there were times when having a fortune would ease her life and the lives of those around her.

Oh, very well, she conceded, she did sometimes wish for the luxuries money could buy. She had grown skilled with a needle and she remade all her gowns. Still, she would not mind having a new gown from an extravagant silk with gold threads woven through it. The blue-and-yellow-striped frock was nice, but it did not shimmer in the light like many of the dresses she had seen this Season.

Money would also allow her to build a place for Mr. Wilkes. Arabella helped Emily negotiate a corner and said, "I feel guilty that Mr. Wilkes started a fire last night in Lady Hector's stables."

"It was unfortunate, but it was only a pile of straw and quickly doused."

"Yes." Arabella chewed at her lower lip. Mr. Wilkes had been abjectly apologetic, but she knew he would be back in the stables again tomorrow working on something else.

"Well, we shall not be here much longer," Emily pointed out optimistically. "Surely he can't do too much damage in the time we have left."

Arabella hoped not. "We are back at Lady Hector's," she told Emily, and together they mounted the steps.

Four hours later, Arabella wore the blue-and-yellow-striped gown on her way to the Manderbys' house. Beside her Lady Hector adjusted her turban more firmly on her head and announced, "Lydia Lancaster is to wed."

"Oh?" Arabella tried to remember who Miss Lancaster was. The debutantes all seemed so much alike. Even their clothes were made by the same fashionable modistes and they spoke in the same cultured accents.

"She is engaged to Lord Coventry." The countess hesitated, then ventured, "Do you mind terribly that you have never wed?"

"No," Arabella said honestly. "I would as lief be on the shelf than unhappily married."

"Sometimes one must be practical about such things," the countess said gently. "One may not love one's husband, but there are advantages to marriage. A woman can have children. My children have been the light of my life."

Arabella suspected Lady Hector had not been happily married. If she had wed the impoverished man she had loved, would she feel differently about marriage? Did the fact the countess sometimes looked wistfully into the distance have anything to do with a man who had been gone from her life for thirty years?

"Wouldn't you like children, dear?" Lady Hector pressed.

"I do like children." The only time Arabella felt true emptiness was when she considered that she would never have any of her own. "I once considered becoming a governess, but that was not possible. I could never abandon Emily and Mr. Wilkes, and no household would accommodate them."

"Emily is a dear child, but there is little real work she can do. As for Mr. Wilkes . . ." Her voice fell away in disapproval.

"He did not mean to start the fire," Arabella said quickly. "It was only a small one and soon put out." Still, she had been horrified to learn of the accident.

"It is not just the fire. That engine he is trying to build is dreadful. It smells when it runs and it does absolutely nothing. He has frightened my servants with his talk of a carriage that runs without being pulled by horses. Can you imagine anything so ridiculous?"

The carriage lurched suddenly and Arabella set her bonnet right before replying. "Actually, Mr. Trevithick did invent a road locomotive early in this century and—"

"It's nonsense, Arabella, and you mustn't encourage him."

"Mr. Wilkes builds his things cheaply. He's always looking about for cast-off parts." Perhaps it was wrong to defend him, but his inventions meant everything to him. He had already lost his wife and both his children. Surely he was entitled to his dreams. Arabella only hoped they didn't result in another fire.

Lady Hector sighed and looked out the carriage. They continued the rest of the way in silence.

Twenty minutes later Arabella and the countess entered a salon of sweeping dimensions. Tiny downward-pointing spires dripped from the ceiling like thick icing from a cake. The walls were painted a deep crimson and embellished around the doorways and windows with cream-colored trim.

The extravagant room provided a backdrop for the ladies' exquisite gowns and massive jewels. Arabella saw that the gentlemen's valets had gone into frenzies of sartorial excitement and dressed their masters in expensive coats and cravats tied in such overblown styles as the Osbaldeston, Trone d'amour, and Maharatta.

Arabella glanced down at her own lemon yellow gown with its coy blue stripes running through it and hoped she was elegant enough for the occasion. She had made the gown last week from an old ballgown that had once belonged to her mother. The simple bodice gave way beneath her bosom to a full, swirling skirt. The gown was becoming, but Arabella knew it was not of the first stare of fashion.

The gentlemen, however, did not appear to care. As soon as she entered the ballroom, she was surrounded by men requesting a dance. She laughed at their pretty words of flattery, enjoying herself far too much to object to harmless flirtation. She even agreed to stand up with Lord Peterby. Of course he held her too closely and pressed her to go into the garden with him, but she cheerfully refused.

Arabella was standing beside Lady Hector, where Lord Peterby had reluctantly deposited her, when Lord Seagraves approached. "You do remember that you have promised me the boulanger, Miss Fairingdale. I was afraid I would be forgotten in the crush of gentlemen."

She smiled ruefully. "Not forgotten." Her legs felt limp and her feet ached. She would have a bruise tomorrow where someone's heavy boot had fallen on her arch. "But I fear I am too exhausted to dance."

"Exhaustion becomes you," he said gallantly. "Your face is flushed and your eyes as bright as stars. I find your enthusiasm refreshing." He dropped his voice to confide, "Some of the young ladies are so demure as to be near death. You always radiate life."

"You are too kind." His friendly smile made his words seem warm and comfortable. She trusted him. He was not bold and calculating like Lord Peterby but sincere and endearingly awkward. She was lucky that he had inherited the property in Kent.

"The Season will end before long," he remarked as he led her toward the refreshment room. "Will you return to Kent immediately?"

Arabella wished she had news from Manchester. She was growing restless with the wait. "I do not know yet. I may be obliged to make a journey north first."

"You are welcome to come to the estate whenever you wish. I took the liberty of inspecting the outside of your house and spied a few missing shingles. I have ordered them replaced."

"How thoughtful," she said gratefully.

He shrugged. "I want the house to be in good repair. When I return to Kent, I shall inspect it more thoroughly and order work on anything that has been neglected."

Arabella looked directly at him. "You cannot imagine how this relieves me." She had spent a good deal of money during her stay in London. Even though she made over her dresses herself, she had purchased many small items. The costs of fans and shawls and gloves had begun to mount.

Arabella and Lord Seagraves were finishing their

refreshments when the partner to whom she had promised the country set came to claim her. After that dance, she returned again to Lady Hector and was standing beside the countess when someone touched her arm.

Arabella turned to face the marquess. She had a vague impression that his clothes were impeccable, but it was the memory of their kiss that made her stiffen.

"Would you rather dance or walk in the garden?" he inquired.

"Which is safer?" she asked warily.

He smiled disarmingly. "Dancing."

It wasn't. The dance was a waltz, and from the moment the music began and he drew her close to him, Arabella realized he did not move with the stiff, precise steps of most gentlemen. He performed the dance with a swift, sure motion that set her striped skirts whirling out about her until the blues and yellows blended into a blur.

She looked at him and demanded, "What news is there of Mr. Bartley?"

"Arabella," he lectured, "when I am dancing with you, you are to be so enthralled with my superior skill that you think of nothing but me."

"Humph." It annoyed her not a little that she *was* thinking of him. She pressed on: "I spoke with Sir David regarding the mill and he had some excellent suggestions."

"Good lord. The man is always on the floor of Parliament giving some impassioned speech or another about the rights of workers. Whatever caused you to speak to him?"

"Because he cares about the rights of workers," she said indignantly. "He gave me books full of new ideas. I have read a great many of them and I have a number of suggestions."

He pulled her to the edge of the floor and out an open door before setting her down beside a long stone balustrade. "You should have consulted with me before running about town asking for advice from men with wild ideas."

"I do not need your permission to do anything. I have always done as I see fit, and I shall continue in that vein." Arabella crossed her arms in defiance and then realized that action had pushed her breasts up dramatically. She immediately let her arms drop to her sides.

He smiled at her with the tolerance a cat might show its wayward kitten. "Don't you ever bend to the wisdom of men?"

Arabella considered the question, then shook her head. "Until Papa died, he was the man whose decisions most affected me. He was a wonderful person, always full of laughter and good humor. But every decision he made was wrong. He was convinced he could invent a machine that would cause water to flow uphill. Why anyone would want one, I do not know. Then he tried to make a pump that would run off air." She sighed. "It never ran at all. We moved from village to village and house to house, and I guess I came to see that even though he was a man, he was not always wise."

The strong lines of his face softened. "Judging from your tone, it does not appear to have diminished your affection for your father."

"Oh, never that. Papa was good and kind. He carved wooden toys for me and played with me when I was young. Maybe in time he would have perfected a pump," she added.

"I think you have inherited your father's determination."

Arabella did not think he meant it unkindly, so

she did not take exception. They seemed to have enough cause to argue without finding new ones.

After a moment of silence, he asked conversationally: "Are you enjoying the Season?"

She looked through the open door at the couples dancing. "More than I ought to."

He chuckled. "You don't have to feel guilty if you are not doing good works every second, Miss Fairingdale. It is perfectly permissible to enjoy yourself."

She cast a sidelong glance at him. "And you? Are you enjoying yourself, milord?" If he was, why did he seldom smile?

He hesitated. "The Season is no longer new to me. I cannot be expected to embrace it with the same fervor I knew when I first came up to London."

She leaped at the opening. "Then perhaps it is time you turned your thoughts toward more important matters. Sir David would be pleased to meet with you and talk with you."

He slanted an ironic smile toward her. "I did not think you could remain off that subject long."

"It is important to me," she said stubbornly.

An anxious-looking man appeared in the doorway. "Miss Fairingdale, the dance is beginning."

Arabella would rather have stayed outside and continued the discussion with the marquess, but that was not to be. She murmured parting words and gave her arm to her partner.

Lord Ridgeton, she noted, remained outside alone. Perhaps he was thinking about what she had said.

Chapter 5

HALF AN hour later, Lord Ridgeton and Lord Peterby left the Manderbys' ball. The marquess guided his sporty curricle out of the St. James's Square area toward a far less desirable part of town.

"Saw you on the balcony with Miss Fair-and-Delightful." The earl smirked. "Did you manage a kiss?"

"No. We acted like mature and responsible people. She told me about her father and his inventions." He, on the other hand, had *not* told her about Harry's troubles. He had not wanted to upset her when they seemed to be at peace with each other. Tomorrow would be soon enough to tell her.

"Dear me, Cedric. You really are becoming a monk. Next you will tell me you harbor nothing except brotherly feelings toward her."

That would be a lie. Lord Ridgeton had looked at the red sheen on Arabella's lips—and he had noticed the white skin of her shoulders. Surely she would feel soft to touch. When she had crossed her arms and revealed a luscious display of wares, he had certainly noticed.

"Men are starting to litter Lady Hector's parlor with increasing frequency. Mr. Hammonds and Sir Wilfred seem quite taken with her. One of them might even offer for her."

"Neither would be any match for a woman of such spirit."

"I quite agree. She would need a strong master. I'm not in the market for a wife, you understand, but I expect there are things I could teach her."

None of them destined to enhance her reputation, Lord Ridgeton knew. "How much further?" he asked in a brisk change of subject.

"Another few blocks."

The subject of Arabella Fairingdale was dropped. Ten minutes later they reached a decaying alehouse, left the curricle with the tiger, and set off down a weed-choked lane.

Lord Ridgeton heard frenzied shouts even before they reached the old barn behind the alehouse. At the door of the barn, the sharp odor of stale horse manure and moldering hay assaulted him. It was a profound change from the expensive Hungary water and rich perfumes that had scented the air at the Manderbys'.

He stepped inside a building hot from too many lanterns. People stood shoulder-to-shoulder. The crowd was half wild with excitement and their unbridled fever nudged his old enthusiasm back to life. He peered over the circle of bent heads to the arena in the center. There, on a battlefield of straw, fierce fighting ensued between a small black cock and a larger russet-colored one. Blood had already begun to flow and one bird's wing dangled uselessly even though the enraged cock flew at its opponent with murderous intent.

"That's a right 'un there!" someone shouted gleefully.

"Hit 'im again!"

Lord Peterby reached into his pocket and withdrew a handful of coins. "Where's the betting?" he demanded of the toothless man next to him.

Lord Ridgeton looked around the low-ceilinged room. Lanterns hung from fat beams and young boys peered down from an opening in the loft. Around him stood a hundred or more men in ragged clothes. Sprinkled among the poor were dandies in impeccable coats and fine twill trousers. They watched the action with practiced indifference, but the marquess knew some had bet next month's income on the fight.

He looked back toward the cocks and saw bright red blood flow. One of the cocks was clearly beginning to falter.

The marquess had not attended a blood sport since before he left for the Continent. As he watched the crippled bird struggle to attack, some of his enthusiasm deserted him. Then the cock began trying to fold into itself in defense against the death blows being dealt it. The rising cheers from the crowd and the wild exhortations washed dully over him.

Standing in the decrepit barn, he recalled the hoarse shouts and terrified screams that had pounded against him in the thick of battle. He thought about the dead littering the battleground after the fighting ended.

A cock screamed in pain.

Suddenly he could not remain in the barn any longer. On the battlefield, he had had no choice but to bear the suffering, but here he could leave.

He pivoted to go.

"What the devil are you doing?" Lord Peterby demanded.

"I'll wait for you outside."

"You can't leave! We just got here."

The marquess ducked to avoid hitting a low beam. An idea had started to form in his head. He must have imbibed more than was good for him at the ball because it was an outrageous idea. Still . . .

"I mean to be here awhile," Lord Peterby shouted after him over the din. "You might as well stay."

He ignored Peterby and pushed through the door to the outside. The idea was fully formed now. Moving with purpose, he went around to the back of the building where an old man and a boy stood guard over two dozen crates of muttering cocks.

"Who's in charge?" Lord Ridgeton demanded.

The old man rose and inspected his visitor in the light from the lantern. Apparently satisfied with what he saw, he nodded politely. "I am, gov'nor."

"How much to buy all your fighters?"

"Buy? Are ye mad?" He raised the lantern to look again. "They aren't for sale."

"Of course they are. Name your price."

The boy watched in openmouthed fascination.

The old man held firm. "People in there are waiting to see a fight. Think 'ow disappointed they'd be, then, if there is none."

"They will find another diversion," the marquess pointed out calmly.

The man peered into his face to determine if he was disguised or deranged. "Is this a jest?"

"You may call it what you wish. As long as you emerge a richer man, what is the difference to you?"

"What indeed?" A crafty smile overtook him. "I would not mind being rich."

The marquess did not intend to make him rich, but after brief negotiations, the old man was smiling with greedy glee. He pocketed the money and turned to the boy. "What are you waiting for? Carry the birds to the gov'nor's coach."

The boy began scooping up wire crates. With a crate under each arm and one dangling from the end of each hand, he headed down the dark lane.

Lord Ridgeton picked up a couple of crates and

followed to the curricle. "Put them there." He indicated the small seat in back where the tiger sat.

The tiger looked at him askance.

"You can hold the crates, Tom," the marquess told the worried tiger.

As the old man and boy loaded the cargo, the marquess stepped back and brushed straw from knee breeches that Weston had labored over for days. He felt satisfied and oddly at peace with himself.

The old man and the boy disappeared back into the darkness. Tom sat ramrod stiff amid the birds flapping in cages around him. The marquess lounged against the curricle and placidly smoked a cheroot.

Within ten minutes, Lord Peterby stomped up. "You won't credit it. There are no more fights. I can scarcely believe it, but some fool—" He stopped dead at the sight of cages stacked high on the backseat. "Have your wits gone begging, Cedric?"

Lord Ridgeton tossed the cheroot down and ground it out with the heel of his boot. "It's only a lark. You needn't be so concerned."

"You call ruining a perfectly good evening a lark?"

"I ought to have told you what I intended." Except that he had had no idea until he acted.

"Yes, you should have." Peterby's irritation faltered. "Are you doing this to put Edwin Morton out of countenance?" He chuckled in spite of himself. "You should have seen the look on his red face when they announced the fights were over. He'd lost heavily on the last round and hoped to recoup his losses on the next. What a splendid jest on him."

"Yes, wasn't it?" The marquess climbed into the curricle and sat in front of the squawking birds and wary tiger. He started the horses back through the tight, dark streets toward his house. He would put the cocks in the stable for the night. Tomorrow he would decide what to do with them. Even if they were slaughtered, it would be more merciful than having them fight to the death.

Beside him, Peterby's appreciation grew with each passing block. "B'gawd, you haven't lost your sense of humor after all, Cedric. I'd begun to fear you'd become a dull stick since your return, but you're just showing your humor and wildness in different ways." He slapped the marquess on the back and chortled. "This is the most diverting thing I've heard of since Anthony dressed up as a female passenger and commandeered the stage to Dover."

"Indeed."

"What say we partake of the pleasures of two very pretty actresses? Wouldn't that put a splendid cap to the evening?"

Lord Ridgeton shook his head. "I shall leave you to enjoy the ladies alone. Perhaps I shall join you later."

Peterby was still laughing as he bounded down out of the curricle in front of the theater to await the end of the final performance. He waved gaily. "Blast, if that isn't the best damn story I've heard in a long time."

As the marquess continued onward, he glanced over his shoulder to see his tiger watching him as if he were a madman. He wondered if the boy was right. The more distance he put between himself and the barn, the more he wondered why he had purchased the birds.

What was wrong with him? He didn't enjoy watching cocks fight, and he didn't derive pleasure at the gaming tables even when he won. He had no desire to indulge himself with an actress this evening or any other evening.

He did, however, long for some companionship. It was a deeper longing that gnawed at him and left him feeling restless and wistful.

When he reached the house in St. James's Square, he guided the horses toward the stables. There he left Tom with instructions to take the crates into the barn.

While the boy moved reluctantly to obey, Cedric thrust his hands into his pockets and started down the cobblestoned lane toward the front of his house. He was far too restless to go to bed.

It was not late, and he knew half a dozen parties were still flourishing. The Manderbys' house was only five doors from his own and he heard lively music coming from the house. He would stop in for a few minutes; it might offer him the diversion he sought.

Arabella left the dance floor after an energetic contra dance and stepped alone out onto the side balcony. The air felt blessedly cool, and she inhaled deeply.

It was late and many of the guests had already left. The dance floor was no longer crowded and the punch had grown warm. Soon she and Lady Hector would return home and she would slip into bed and review all the delightful moments of the ball.

Arabella had known from the beginning that London and the fast gaiety of the balls was only temporary. Now that her time was drawing to a close, she savored every moment. Perhaps it was selfish—since her first concern ought to be the workers in Manchester—but she did love the parties and the fun.

"Arabella?"

Startled, she turned to see Lord Ridgeton regarding her from the doorway. He had left the party much earlier. She wondered why he had returned.

"I did not think to find you alone." He walked toward her.

"I wanted to rest. I have danced so much that I doubt I shall ever walk again." She did not want him to think she had stood alone and unnoticed the whole time he was gone.

His clothes, she noted now that he was closer, were rumpled. When he stopped beside her, she smelled something wild and barnyardy. His hair looked disheveled and he drummed long fingers against his thigh. How curious.

"Is anything amiss?" she asked.

"No, nothing."

Arabella shook her head at his denial. "You're overset by something. I see it in your countenance." The furrow on his forehead was not usually there.

A slow grin took possession of his face. "I hope Lady Hector does not mean to take you in hand and teach you to coo and simper. There ought to be at least one lady each Season who has a mind of her own."

Arabella couldn't repress a smile. "Milord, all women have minds of their own." She gestured back through the open doors. "The most demure young lady in that ballroom is actually thinking how she is going to hang new draperies throughout milord's mansion once it is hers."

He lifted an eyebrow in horror. "Do you mean young ladies are capable of deceiving gentlemen in order to win a fine house and a title?"

"Only for a gentleman's own good," Arabella pointed out reasonably. "The old pile probably needs new draperies and perhaps a new settee or so."

" 'Tis frightening to think a gentleman is not safe with any woman," he parried.

The teasing tone was still there, but she sensed something new and more subtle between them. Feeling suddenly uncertain, Arabella took a step away. "It has been a marvelous evening. It is too bad you were not able to enjoy all of it." She did not wish to ask outright where he had gone, but she left the door open for him to volunteer.

"I had other business to attend to," he said vaguely.

"Have you heard nothing from Mr. Bartley?" He had not replied when she'd asked him earlier.

He glanced away from her. "There has been a small complication concerning Mr. Bartley."

"Is he ill?" Why was he hesitating?

"No, he is not ill." He brushed his fingers through his hair and a piece of what looked like straw fell out. "He is in jail."

She stared at him. "For what? Surely he did not rob anyone or harm anyone. He does not seem the sort."

"I do not have any particulars yet."

"Jail," she murmured, and thought back to the rotund, inept man who had partnered her about the dance floor. He had done something foolish, of course. Hadn't everyone said he was scatter-brained? "He has done something ridiculous, hasn't he?"

"It's possible."

"It's very probable!" she snapped. "This is dreadfully inconvenient."

The marquess smiled without humor. "I daresay Harry finds it inconvenient as well. Rats and rancid food were never to his liking."

Arabella's anger faltered at the thought of anyone enduring such conditions. "Dear me. Is it as bad as all that?"

"Perhaps not, but something must be done. Harry won't like being confined even if it's in the best of jails."

"What do you mean to do?" Arabella asked.

He finally looked back at her. "I shall have to see to his release."

"Then you are going to Manchester yourself?" Her voice quickened.

"Yes. I shall start the day after tomorrow."

"I shall accompany you. We can survey the mill while we are there."

"Miss Fairingdale—"

Her thoughts raced ahead. "My carriage is not conducive to comfortable travel. I would prefer to ride with you if you have no objections."

"Arabella—"

She heard him but kept talking anyway. "It will serve no purpose to tell me you don't wish me to go. I already *know* you don't want me, but I shall follow in my own coach if I'm not allowed to ride in yours." Arabella hoped it did not come to that. It would be a wearisome, jolting journey in her ramshackle vehicle. However, she gave no indication of that as she gazed at him with steady challenge.

A dark flush of exasperation stained his cheeks. "It is out of the question for you to go."

"Why?"

"It is a long journey."

"Pooh! I was traveling when I was still learning to walk. I've been across the country and back dozens of times. I enjoy travel."

"This is not a trip for pleasure," he shot back. "I am going to free Harry and shall have no time to worry about you. You will have to trust me to do what is best."

"Why?" she challenged. "You haven't been very trustworthy until now. You promised to tell me before your man left and you didn't. Now that you are going, I see no reason I cannot accompany you."

"This is preposterous," he muttered to some invisible person.

She drew herself up stiffly. "You cannot stop me. I mean to go even if I have to take the common stage."

They stood locked in tense silence. His eyes blazed back disapproval at her, and she shot an unflinching look back at him.

At length, he said grudgingly, "If I take you, I shall not stop for you to see the views or shop in the villages."

"I shouldn't expect you to."

"We shall rise early each day and drive until late," he warned.

"Excellent, then we shall arrive all the sooner. You needn't worry that I will interfere with you. I shall bring books to read and amuse myself. You will scarcely know I am there."

Sardonic humor licked at his oak brown eyes. "I shall know you are there every moment."

Arabella did not think he meant it as a compliment, but the underlying tone to his voice was not entirely anger. She was still a woman, and she thought he noticed the things about her that other men noticed. In the confines of a closed carriage, they would certainly be aware of each other, for better or for worse.

It did not matter how comfortable or uncomfortable the journey with him was. The important thing was that she would be able to show him the mill and make him see with his own eyes what she knew. It was unworthy to be glad of someone else's misfortune, but Harry landing in jail might be the best thing that had happened in a long time.

Late in the afternoon of the following day, Lord Ridgeton arrived at his grandmother's house. Her health prevented her from attending the balls and fetes, but she had a wide circle of friends and she seldom lacked company.

At the moment, however, her parlor stood empty save for him and her. The dowager countess sat in a plum-colored damask chair with her arms resting on the wooden arms.

"The word is all over town about you spoiling Edwin Morton's fun by removing a passel of cocks from a barn, Cedric."

He looked at her wizened face with banked amusement. "Grandmama, where do you go to hear such tales? I swear I sometimes think you frequent gambling halls or some other dens of iniquity."

She drew her tiny frame up haughtily. "I have no need to visit such places, although I have no doubt you are familiar with them. Your stunt was the talk of my little parlor this morning." She sniffed daintily. "I almost felt called upon to defend you."

He chuckled. "I hope you were not forced to go that far."

"No, I restrained myself."

Leaning back in his chair, he crossed one long leg over the other. "Do you think me wicked for playing such a jest?" he asked.

"I don't believe it was a jest, Cedric."

"Everyone else thinks it was," he said mildly. She had always had a perception beyond that of ordinary people. A few had said she was fey, but the marquess thought she was just damned shrewd.

She sniffed. "Everyone else is a fool."

"Not a very kind thing to say about London society." He reproved her in an amused voice.

"Don't come the innocent with me, boy. I've still got my wits. I see that you've changed." She stared at him, daring him to argue.

He waited. His grandmother would not have called him here unless she wished to deliver herself of an opinion—of which she was known to have many—or unless she wished to give him a dressing down.

"You're not a hellion anymore, Cedric. You've grown more thoughtful. I'll wager you're ready to give up your old ways for good."

The fact he had reflected on those very things about himself did not make him agree with her. He held his silence and waited to see where the conversation was headed.

"I've seen it happen dozens of times before. When a man tires of watching birds beat each other to death, and when he no longer wishes to spend his time with high flyers, he's ready for something more serious. Matrimony," she concluded, with a sage nod.

The marquess smiled indulgently. "Grandmama, you are making a grand leap from rescuing a few birds to determining it is time to get myself shackled."

"Plenty of gels out there to choose from," she continued, undeterred. "Dozens of them would give their right arm to have you."

"I would rather marry a woman with all her limbs," he noted drily.

The tiny woman shot him a quelling look. "Your poor mama has waited long enough for you to wed. It's past time to act. This Season is the time."

He shook his head. "I fear I must disappoint you.

I am leaving town tomorrow and I doubt I shall return before the Season ends."

She pursed her lips into a tight, disapproving pucker. "What is there to draw you from London at the height of the Season?"

"Business."

"Stuff! Miss Serena Morris has already turned down a score of offers. I would not depend on her to wait for you until next Season—even though you are her first choice."

Rising, he bent to drop a kiss on her frail cheek.

"Are you leaving?" she demanded.

"Yes. Otherwise, you will have old Winters come in here and carve out my liver."

"It would be nothing less than you deserve."

"You may be right." He lifted her shawl from where it had slipped down behind her and placed it securely on her bent shoulders. "You're still the most beautiful woman of them all, Grandmama."

The old woman fought back a smile but lost. "You can be charming when you wish, you wretch. You must put that charm to better use from now on. You must find a bride. Your mother is having a house party shortly after the Season ends. You can choose a bride there."

Lord Ridgeton thought it time to change the subject. "Before I consider a bride, Grandmama, I must decide what to do with the cocks. Their cackling is making the horses restless and the stablehands are insulted. I shall have to go to the expense and inconvenience of sending them to the country. I was foolish to buy them." He paused before adding reflectively, "I daresay I would do it over again."

She nodded with composure, as if his words made perfectly good sense. That didn't seem possible, since they did not even make sense to him. "Yes, it's time," she murmured peacefully.

It struck him that she might be right. For three months he had tried to settle back into a life that no longer suited him. Maybe he was wrong to think he could go back. He must go forward. Was the next step marriage to an acceptable woman?

Lord Ridgeton drove away from his grandmother's house with a great deal to ponder.

Arabella slept little the night of the Manderbys' ball. She tried not to think about the confrontation she had had with Lord Ridgeton. Rather, she concentrated on Harry Bartley. She felt sorry for the clumsy man when she thought of him in jail. Mostly, though, she was dismayed that more time had passed and nothing had been accomplished about the mill. If only the marquess had gone to Manchester in the beginning, she could have been saved all this turmoil.

Stubborn man, she thought as she rolled over and thumped her pillow. Why had he returned to the Manderbys' ball seeming introspective and subdued? Why did he have to have those piercing brown eyes that could sear her or soften her?

Arabella fell asleep amid a tangle of covers without resolving that question.

The next morning she tumbled out of bed ready to begin preparations for her journey. She and Emily were packing gowns when Arabella spied Mr. Wilkes out the back window. His three-cornered hat was pushed far back on his gray hair as he stepped off a distance on the ground in front of the stables. She watched him pace back and forth and scratch his ear the way he always did when he was deep in concentration.

"Oh, dear," Arabella said aloud.

Emily looked up from a green muslin she was folding. "What's wrong?"

"Mr. Wilkes has some invention in mind. He is measuring outside the stables."

"Oh, dear," Emily echoed.

Arabella sighed. She had intended to leave Mr. Wilkes behind while they went to Manchester. Now she realized she could not leave him here to blow the roof off the stables or try to harness the countess's hapless horses to a flight machine. She fingered the lace on her collar and said, "I shall have to take Mr. Wilkes to Manchester with us."

"Will Lord Ridgeton agree to that?"

Arabella turned away from the window and spoke with a confidence she was far from possessing. "He ought to be pleased. After all, Mr. Wilkes can relieve the marquess's driver and help tend the horses in the evenings."

"Yesss." Emily drew the word out doubtfully.

Arabella knew that Lord Ridgeton expected her to bring a maid, but she suspected he would be put out of countenance by the knowledge she was bringing another servant. The easiest course, she decided cravenly, was to say nothing and take Mr. Wilkes with her. If Lord Ridgeton objected, she would have to brazen it out then.

"Is it time for you to dress for callers?" Emily asked.

"Yes." Her companion's sense of time had grown more acute as her vision failed. Arabella left the packing to Emily while she donned a pearl gray gown with white trim around the cap sleeves and square neckline. She brushed her hair back vigorously, but a few defiant curls fought their way forward again. Resigned, Arabella let them have their way and went downstairs to join Lady Hector in the front parlor.

In addition to Lady Hector's old friends who came to call, there were a gratifying number of gentlemen. The men asked polite questions of the countess, but their glances kept straying to Arabella.

"Well," Lady Hector said, with undisguised satisfaction, when they were alone in the parlor. "You have caught the eye of several men. Surely this makes you want to reconsider your decision to leave? . . ."

Arabella shook her head. "No. I am flattered, but I feel no interest in any of them."

"Sir Wilfred is quite charming . . . even though he is a bit old for you," the countess pressed.

"Mr. Hammonds is also old."

"Well, there is still Lord Hargrave. Isn't he enough to keep you from going to Manchester?"

"No. I didn't come to London seeking a husband, and if I had it would not be Lord Hargrave. He has absolutely nothing to say for himself. He asked twice about the weather and twice if I received his flowers."

"He is only a little shy."

"He is boring."

"You are too hard on him. No man is perfect."

Arabella privately agreed. That was probably the reason that she was still unwed. She did not want to pass her days with a man lacking in conversation, wit, or charm.

She was glad when the arrival of another caller put an end to their conversation. Lord Seagraves was dressed in a yellow coat of a brightness that did not seem to match his mood. In point of fact, Arabella thought the earl seemed sad and rather lost. His long face looked even more woebegone than usual today.

While the countess poured tea, he confided, "I did not know it would be so difficult to reenter society. I have been invited to an occasional rout, but not everyone greets me warmly. I daresay I have lived away too long and no longer know how to conduct myself in society. I am trying to be an Englishman again, but I do not know if I am succeeding."

"Of course you are succeeding," Lady Hector assured him warmly.

Arabella nodded. It was true she did not see Lord Seagraves often at the events she and Lady Hector attended. It was also true he danced with a heavy step and his accent had been corrupted from living too long in the Colonies. Yes, she had heard uncharitable comments about him, but she did not believe them. He was unfailingly courteous and attentive to her and Lady Hector whenever they met. The fact he was permitting Arabella to retain her house was certainly proof of his generosity. It made her angry to think of such a kind person being treated badly by his countrymen.

"It must be a relief to return home after living among savages," Lady Hector noted, and looked at him with eager expectation.

"Hardly savages. Charleston is a refined town—full of the comforts and conveniences of England."

"Oh," she said flatly.

Arabella smothered a smile at Lady Hector's disappointment that she was not to be regaled with tales of maraudering Indians and wild settlers.

"Charleston is a beautiful city; I miss it. Of course," he added, "I am glad to be back in England. I daresay the longer I am here, the warmer people will become toward me. Within a few weeks, I shall be settled in Baxter House and living the life of a country gentleman as if I had never left." He plucked at a loose thread on his knee breeches and looked even more morose.

Why had he left? Arabella wondered. She had heard about his father's indiscretions and some vague rumors about Lord Seagraves himself. If there was anything untoward in his past, however, she was sure it had been caused by a boyish energy that had been tempered by maturity. She could not imagine him embroiled in anything unsavory.

"I shall return to my home in the country soon, too," Lady Hector said. "I look forward to seeing my dear little grandchildren again and being in my own house."

Arabella felt a twinge of something foreign to her. She would return to the house at the back of the Baxter estate, but she did not truly have a home. Arabella did not require an opulent mansion, but there would be a comfort to having her own address and in knowing she could never be asked to leave.

"You are quiet, Miss Fairingdale," Lord Seagraves noted.

She smiled. "I am tired after last night's soiree. I do not keep such late hours in Kent and am unaccustomed to so much activity."

"Kent will undoubtedly seem boring to you when you return. We must see what we can do to change that."

He smiled at her with such benevolence that Arabella felt guilty for wishing for her own home. Lord Seagraves was generous to offer her the house. She should be grateful instead of wishing for more than she could ever have.

"I hope to entertain more than my aunt did," Lord Seagraves continued.

"That will be so nice," Lady Hector said enthusiastically. "Arabella has enjoyed the amusements here in London; I dislike thinking of her being without diversion in the country."

He paused uncertainly, then confided, "I have been so long away . . . I am not certain I know how to entertain. I shall depend on Miss Fairingdale to introduce me to the local society."

"I am sure she will be delighted to help you."

Arabella nodded. "Certainly. Once I return to Kent, I shall be glad to assist." Not that she imagined he should need her help. The master of Baxter House would have admittance to any house he desired. Invitations were probably already pouring in. It was only in London that people were stupidly rude. "At the moment, however, I do not know when I shall reach Kent." Depending on what she saw in Manchester, Arabella might feel compelled to remain there awhile.

"I hope you are not away long. I count you one of the few friends I have in England. Certainly you are one of the few people I know near Baxter House. I wish to be able to call on you for conversation and advice."

It was nice to be needed. Arabella had feared she would feel without purpose without Lady Baxter. "You may call on me whenever you wish."

He thanked her warmly and left wearing a pleased expression.

"Such a pleasant man," Lady Hector noted after he was gone.

"Yes." Arabella traced a finger around the trim of her neckline. "I wonder why he went to the Colonies and stayed away so long."

"Some minor scandal. Some people believe him to be without scruples, but no one can give me any examples."

"There are always rumors about people," Arabella said. She saw nothing in his conduct to suggest he had ever been anything but respectable.

Rising, she picked up her fan. "I must see to my packing. We leave early in the morning."

Chapter 6

THE FOLLOWING day, the marquess sat facing Arabella and her companion as his well-sprung chaise rolled northward. It was late morning and Miss Emily Windell had fallen asleep and lay slumped against Arabella's shoulder.

Lord Ridgeton watched Arabella try to nudge her companion back toward her side of the carriage. She shifted her shoulder and pursed her lips with the effort, but it proved a hopeless task. Miss Windell only sighed and sank, once again, toward the soft comfort of Arabella's side.

He doubted even the weight of her companion would diminish Arabella's enthusiasm. When she had greeted him this morning, her eyes had shone a rich, dazzling blue. She had smiled constantly while the trunks and valises were being loaded. Her coachman, the peculiar man with the tricorn hat, had assisted. Arabella had murmured something about him, but the marquess hadn't heard her over the neighing and pawing of the restless horses.

Now, as the carriage jolted over a rough patch of road, he watched Miss Windell sink heavily against her mistress. Arabella tried again to push her back, but the sleeping woman only snored unresponsively.

He suppressed a smile. "It would appear your

companion is determined to occupy the whole of the seat. Why do you not sit beside me?"

She looked at him gratefully. "Would you mind?"

"Not in the least." He would not have offered if he had minded. He was not in the habit of burdening himself with things he did not wish to do—excepting, of course, making this trip. Even that was not causing him undue hardship. After all, he had no reason to remain in London. He had found little enjoyment there.

Arabella picked up her skirts and kept her head low as she moved over to sit beside him. Emily immediately sank down until the side of her face pressed against the soft squabs of the elegant traveling carriage. Once seated beside Lord Ridgeton, Arabella gave him a quick, thankful smile, then flipped her guidebook open and began reading.

The rocking motion of the carriage continued as Lord Ridgeton opened the window a small space and looked out. He saw green fields and ancient stands of trees alongside a river that glittered golden in the morning sun. A man herded some goats down the road past him and some workers in the field were stopping to sit under the shade of a tree. It was a peaceful scene that made him feel at ease with the world.

He glanced over and saw Arabella still reading from her guidebook. "What does it say?" he asked.

She put her index finger in the book to hold her place. "We are passing near St. Albans. The city is eighteen hundred years old and was the site of Verulamium, one of the finest Roman towns in Britain." She looked at him. "Don't you find something powerful about a part of the country so immersed in history?"

"All of Britain is old. The druids skulked about the Salisbury Plains long before the Romans came."

"Yes, I suppose you are right." She looked thoughtfully into the distance.

He followed her gaze and saw the top of a red brick tower perched on a hill above some green beech trees. A half-timbered house slid past his view and then all was green again.

"Don't you wonder what the Ancients were like and what they thought?" Arabella asked pensively.

He had never wondered before now, but the faraway sound of her voice and her wistful expression made him pause to think. "I suppose they were not so very different from you and me."

"Hmmm." She looked back down at the book and began to read again. "The book says the county lacks durable stone for building. Most of the stone is chalk with a bit of clay in the river valleys. I suppose that is why the houses are made of thatch and tiles."

"I daresay."

They drifted off into silence and she continued reading the book while he gazed out the window.

His thoughts turned from the scenery to more practical matters. A wife, his grandmother had said. She had always spoken her mind plainly, but she was also a wise woman. It was, he acknowledged, time to consider marriage and heirs. He reviewed in his mind all the young ladies he recalled meeting this Season. It was hard going to put names with faces. He was more likely to remember a pretty smile, or a witty bit of conversation, or the feel of an especially smooth silk gown. Yet there was nothing distinctive enough about any one woman to make him want to court her seriously.

Was he being too particular?

He did not think so. With his fortune and title, he could expect the best. He immodestly reflected that he was also possessed of a strong body and a quick mind. He deserved the most beautiful, accomplished, rich woman the Season offered. That would be Serena Morris, but he had been profoundly disinterested in her.

He felt a touch on his shoulder and looked over to see Arabella crumpling against his side. Her head fell slowly until her chin came to rest on the shelf of his shoulder. Her sleeping breath blew soft and warm against his cravat. A slow, heated feeling uncurled inside him. He smelled lavender on her clothes, and he saw the thick sweep of her eyelashes as they laid curling upward, away from the white satin of her cheeks.

Abruptly he turned to face ahead. He was going to marry a society chit, so it was inconsequential that Arabella Fairingdale's laughter lifted upward at the end or that her skin was as smooth as the tender new leaves that uncurled on the lime trees each spring. The blasted truth was that she had been disarmingly pleasant all morning. He was coming to like her, and that made it difficult for him to maintain an impassive demeanor toward her.

There was, he supposed, nothing wrong with being friendly with Arabella, but that was where it must stop. He was not some rake like Peterby who would try to push that friendship further.

Lord Ridgeton looked back at Arabella just as she murmured sleepily and settled more firmly against his shoulder. Her small green bonnet had slipped aside; only thin ribbons tied around her neck kept the bonnet from falling to the floor. Her hair was a tumbled array of flaxen ringlets and curling wisps that begged to be smoothed down.

He kept his hands resolutely at his side and looked away.

A moment later the carriage hit a ferocious bump; Arabella slid off his shoulder and fell toward the floor. He lunged forward and caught her, holding her tentatively as he tried to decide what to do. Her mouth, he noted, was very close to his. A man of fewer scruples might have taken advantage of the moment. Fortunately he was a gentleman.

With a gentleman's resolve, he determined to prop her in the corner. He dipped her carefully backward to position her against the side of the carriage.

At that moment they hit another hard bump that sent him up off the seat and she with him. Instinctively he tightened his grip about her slender shoulders. She whimpered in sleepy protest before her head fell forward against his neck. Her hair rubbed softly against his chin and her mouth fitted snugly into his cravat at the hollow of his throat. He swallowed heavily.

This would not do at all.

Moving with care and deliberation, he attempted to shift her away from him. He was halfway there when he felt her stir, then stiffen.

"Lord Ridgeton?" she gasped.

He looked down into a pair of startled eyes and thought irrelevantly that they were the color of pure, deep water.

"W-What are you doing?"

"Protecting you."

She blinked uncertainly. "Protecting me from what?"

From me, he almost said. Instead he replied with dignity: "You fell asleep, Miss Fairingdale, and were toppling forward. I saved you from falling."

"Oh, I see." She watched him uncertainly.

"I am sorry if I alarmed you." Suddenly aware that he still clutched her against him, he released her. Why the devil hadn't he done that the moment she woke up?

"You did alarm me," she confessed, and reached up to pull her bonnet back into place.

"I apologize," he said stiffly.

She smiled with a returning confidence. "It was confusing to awaken and not know where I was or who was holding me. But I am fully awake now and we must not make too much of it."

Lord Ridgeton didn't reply. He was aware of a need to maintain barriers, even if she was not.

Arabella retied the dainty satin strings. "I shall be glad to reach Manchester. I know you believe I have been stubborn and unnecessarily insistent, but once you see the conditions at the mill, you will come round to my way of thinking."

A slow smile stretched across his face. "You prefer it when others agree with you, do you not?"

"Only when I am right." Her words were pious, but an impish light shone in her eyes.

He gave a bark of laughter.

Arabella pressed a slender index finger to her lips."Shhh. You'll awaken Emily."

"My dear," he drawled, "the end of the world would not awaken your companion."

"She *can* be a sound sleeper." Arabella looked fondly at Emily, and the marquess realized this was more than a servant. She was also Arabella's friend.

"Has Miss Windell been with you long?" he asked to bring the conversation into neutral territory.

"Three years. She was turned off from her last job as a governess because her eyesight was failing. When she could no longer read the words on the page, she began making up stories for the children. They were exciting stories about damsels and dragons and wizards. At first, no one noticed her poor eyesight and her employers were content, but eventually it became known." Arabella sighed. "It's difficult to hide such a thing when you are bumping into the furniture and when the children began to replace themselves in their beds with their dolls and race around downstairs unsupervised."

"Little urchins."

"I suppose you were a saint as a child?"

"Of course."

She smirked.

"Actually," he informed her, "I was a relatively obedient child. It was not until I went to London as a young man that I grew less restrained."

"Why?"

The directness of her question caught him unaware. He hesitated before replying, "For the usual reasons. Every young man indulges himself when he first tastes freedom."

She shook her head. "No, such wildness is an affliction known only to rich young men. Common laborers and country farmers are steady and responsible by the time they turn fourteen. I was not much older than that when I matured." She thought about that and chuckled. "Or *thought* I was mature. Papa did not think me so sophisticated. He said I was putting on airs."

"You must have been a handful for your poor papa."

"I fear I was," she agreed ruefully. Shaking her head, she said, "I do not know how the subject turned to me. We were discussing how Emily became my companion. She was turned off from her employment and had nowhere else to go. I was in need of a companion."

"Who lived with you before that?"

"A genteel elderly woman." Arabella lowered her voice. "I think she was scandalized by me. She was so pleased when the vicar offered for me," she continued in a talkative vein, "I don't think she ever forgave me for turning him down."

"There were surely other suitors," he said casually. "A Frenchman with a balloon, I believe?" Harry had once said as much. At the time the marquess had not cared; now he wanted to know more.

She blushed. "So you have heard of him. He was not really a suitor. Well, he *did* make a proposal, but it was not a proper one."

The atmosphere in the carriage suddenly felt heavy, like the weight of the air before a storm. "The blackguard." He was surprised at the cold anger coursing through him.

"I called him worse at the time, but he is French, you see, so it did not disturb him overmuch."

Her acceptance at having received an improper advance only raised the marquess's anger higher. "You should have had him dispatched to the beyond," he grumbled.

"I am not very good with a pistol," Arabella said. "I daresay Mr. Wilkes would have fought a duel for me, but his reflexes have not been good since he turned seventy. I do not think he was a terribly good shot even in his younger days."

The marquess sat mute, struck by the realization there was no one to protect Arabella's honor. Any man who chose to insult her was free to do so. He had known all along that she had no protector; but this incident brought home how fragile and alone she was. A woman like Arabella, for all her fire, was still a woman.

The cooling voice of reason warned him if he was going to travel in a closed vehicle with her for the next several days, he must not dwell too much on the feminine side of her. He would protect her, of course, if necessary, but that was where his concern for her ended. He would do well to remember that.

* * *

Shortly after noontime they stopped for lunch. Arabella's legs felt as soft as dough as she climbed down out of the carriage. She took Emily's arm partly to help Emily and partly to keep herself upright. They were starting for the inn when Arabella saw the marquess frowning at Mr. Wilkes.

Lord Ridgeton turned toward her. "Why is that man with us?"

Oh, dear. They were not so far from London that the marquess could not send Mr. Wilkes back. She smiled graciously. "He is helping your driver. Surely you recall that I told you as much this morning?"

His frown deepened until it etched two parallel lines between his eyebrows. "You mumbled *something*, but I did not hear you."

Now was not the time to admit guilt. Arabella blinked innocently. She could not be blamed for noises the horses had made. What was she to do if her voice had fallen soft just when she was explaining about Mr. Wilkes?

"Well, he is here now," he mumbled gracelessly. "Charles is already sitting up front against his wishes. The addition of your man makes it quite crowded up there."

"I'm so sorry." Arabella tried to put sincerity into the words. She could hardly explain that she had been forced to bring Mr. Wilkes along so he didn't destroy London while she was away. She doubted the knowledge Mr. Wilkes was a dangerous man would soothe the marquess.

She skirted the matter altogether by saying, "I hope they have some agreeable food at this inn, don't you?"

He nodded without interest.

Arabella was glad the matter of Mr. Wilkes had been laid to rest. It was unfair of her to have brought him without having Lord Ridgeton's permission, but she had had no choice.

She and Emily continued toward the inn.

"Lord Ridgeton sounded unhappy," Emily said as Arabella reached for the door handle.

"Yes." She sighed. "I shall have to be excessively agreeable the rest of the trip to make up for the inconvenience." Actually she did not think it would prove so onerous to be agreeable to the marquess. He was showing himself to be a good traveling companion. There had been that rather awkward moment when she had awakened to find him holding her, but he had acted out of necessity. It was too bad of her to have noticed the uncompromising strength of his arms. But she thought she had recovered well, and they were on friendly but correct terms with each other.

Emily chose to eat in the sun while Arabella enjoyed a simple meal of bread and cheese and apples with Lord Ridgeton in a small room off the ale hall.

As she reached for the cheese, Arabella asked him pleasantly, "How far do you think we shall travel today?"

"I hope to reach Wilmingham Hall this afternoon and spend the night there with my friend."

She nodded. The wine felt cool in her throat and would help her sleep again once they began to drive. She would sit beside Emily—so she did not end up in the marquess's arms again! "I must read in my guidebook about the house, so I can sound intelligent and charming when I meet your friend."

Lord Ridgeton snorted. "The guidebook will doubtless say it is distinguished. It's not. It's an ugly old pile that ought to be pulled down. The moat has been filled in with gardens, but that is the only redeeming quality. Still, Sir William is an old friend from my days at Eton and he would be hurt if I did not stop to see him."

"Of course." Lord Ridgeton must have rich friends scattered across the country. It occurred to her that he could stay wherever he wished for however long he wished. There were definite advantages to being well connected.

A short time later they were traveling again and the wine quickly put Arabella to sleep.

Sometime in the late afternoon the carriage jostled to a stop. She blinked awake and looked out at a gray building of graceless proportions. The encircling shrubbery surely marked the spot where the moat had stood. Deep gashes of windows sat far back into the building. The marquess had been right to declare it ugly.

Within moments the party stood in a vaulted great hall. A menacing boar's head with flaring nostrils threatened them from above the gigantic fireplace.

Tall, red-haired Sir William greeted them warmly. After introductions were made, Arabella followed a servant up a wide staircase. Her room was big and drafty, but it overlooked a lush grove of trees where a chorus of birds sang. Arabella bathed and took a brief nap before dinner.

Emily helped Arabella dress in a flowing blue frock. Then Arabella joined the men in a long room punctured with windows.

Behind Sir William's cheery cordiality, she sensed his curiosity about her. Lady Hector had warned her that people would talk, but she did not believe her reputation would suffer. Only an excessively stupid person would believe the marquess had a romantic interest in her.

"We have little company here and the cook has taken the opportunity to prepare a feast. I hope you are very hungry," Sir William said as he escorted her down a long hall to the dining room.

It was only the three of them and a crowd of servants in a dining room that shanked off the main portion of the house like a foot kicking out from the bulky body of the house. Sir William seated her in the center of the table, then he and the marquess took places at either end.

"Lord Ridgeton tells me you are fresh from the London Season, Miss Fairingdale."

"Yes. It was my first."

Surprise flickered across his face.

Smothering a laugh, she explained, "I was not being presented."

"You most assuredly could be, Miss Fairingdale. You look quite young enough," he said, rallying gallantly.

She was eight years too old, but she did not quibble. She knew she did not look like a girl, but the cheval glass had told her she looked smart and pretty in the blue gown that moved like a curtain in a soft breeze. Her hair was a bouquet of curls. Even the marquess had taken a second look when she had entered the room.

"I hope you will remain a few days. You will want to rest and enjoy the countryside," Sir William said as servants cleared one set of dishes and placed a barrage of new covers before them.

Lord Ridgeton shook his head. "It will not be possible to remain beyond tonight."

"You must not rush Miss Fairingdale across the land without giving her a chance to enjoy it," Sir William said, chiding him.

The marquess laughed. "You do not understand who is rushing whom."

"I am the one who is in a hurry to reach Manchester," Arabella explained. "Lord Ridgeton and I have urgent business there."

"It sounds very serious."

"Yes, we shall leave rather early in the morning," Lord Ridgeton said.

"Surely not before touring the grounds and the deer park, Miss Fairingdale?"

Arabella smiled apologetically. "I am afraid we must press on."

"Of course," he said politely.

The rest of the meal passed in a flow of courses and easy conversation between Sir William and the marquess. She listened to their talk of old friends and answered Sir William's polite questions to her. She knew, though, that she was fading. The large canopied bed in her room seemed to call to her. The sheets had looked clean and soft and the bedclothes thick enough to warm her against the night air.

She was glad when she was able to retire to her room, slip out of her blue frock, and crawl into bed in her chemise.

Fragments of the day's events flitted in and out of her mind, but she was too tired to concentrate on them. It was good to lie still after the day-long movement of the carriage. She was sliding toward sleep almost the moment her head touched the pillow.

Arabella did not know what caused her to awaken some time later. It was not the sound of the insects, although they did chirp loudly. Nor was it the wind blowing whispers through the larches. It might have been a noise in the passage, but she could not think who would be up at this hour. Then she heard the sound of a door closing.

Fully awake, she sat up. She heard the noise again.

Slipping from her bed, Arabella went to the window to look out. Below a half-moon an animal scampered out of the shrubberies and across the wide lawn. Perhaps that was what she had heard. She was turning back to her bed when a light came on in the stables. She paused. It seemed very late for anyone to be working.

Well, it wasn't her concern. Chilled, she wrapped her arms around her shoulders and started back to the warm bed. She was in the middle of the dark room when she stopped in midstep. Who would be working in the stables at this late hour? The person who came immediately to mind was her own Mr. Wilkes. He had been known to arise from his bed in the middle of the night when inspiration struck him. Heaven help her if he was inspired!

There was nothing to do but to go see. Sighing, Arabella felt around in the dark until she located the tinderbox and candle beside her bed. She lit the candle, tossed her pelisse over her chemise, and pulled on her half boots.

She tried for quiet as she moved down the dark passages guided only by her wavering candle. Boards groaned underfoot and creaking doors shouted of her presence. She winced at each sound but kept going until she found a door leading out the back. Once outside the house, she abandoned all pretense of stealth and hurried across the damp grass toward the stables.

She pushed back the door and saw a dozen startled horses staring at her over the gates of their stalls. Ignoring them, she headed toward the room where the light shone. She smelled something burning and quickened her steps.

Arabella rushed into the room and collided squarely with a man's body. Dazed, she stood a moment with her cheek pressing into a button. This body was too tall and muscular to belong to Mr. Wilkes.

And that scent of fresh soap and expensive port . . . She stepped back and looked up into Lord Ridgeton's face.

"Good evening, Arabella," he said calmly.

He held a cheroot in his hand, she noted absently. "What are you doing here?" she demanded.

"I might ask you the same thing."

"I saw a light and thought I should investigate." That was part of the truth, she reasoned as she glanced at the harnesses hanging above the wooden benches that lined the walls.

"I came out here to smoke where I would not disturb the household."

"Oh." She stood uncertainly in the doorway. Her warm bed awaited her, but she was suddenly reluctant to leave. She sensed that he, like she, was not telling the whole truth. "Is anything wrong, milord?"

He hesitated. His face no longer looked so impassive. There was even a hint of pain in the brown eyes.

Arabella patted down her tumbled hair. "I do not mean to pry, but I should be glad to listen."

The marquess's clothes, she noted, were wrinkled, as if he had pulled them back on after retiring for the evening. One of the buttons was fastened into the wrong hole. His valet, Charles, would be mortified.

"I do not always sleep well," he said. "I haven't since my return from the campaigns." He stopped as if he were embarrassed at having said that much.

"Do you have bad dreams?"

"Sometimes."

She nodded. "I understand. I had nightmares after Mama's death when I was nine."

"Did they finally go away?" He held the cheroot at his side and sat on one of the benches.

"Yes. Every time I woke up from a nightmare, Papa would take me into the kitchen and give me warm milk and hold me until I felt better. It helped to be soothed and petted."

A wry smile twisted his mouth. "I'm a bit old for that."

She drew the pelisse closer around her. "You probably wouldn't enjoy the warm milk, but one is never too old to be comforted. When you have a bad night, you could awaken Charles and tell him you need to talk."

"Men don't do such things," he informed her.

"They should. Why should you be ashamed of being lonely or afraid? Having someone to talk to would be better than sitting out here alone."

A smile turned the corners of his mouth upward. "I didn't intend to be discovered. I still don't know why you came. Are you also having difficulty sleeping?"

"A noise awoke me. I daresay I heard you leaving the house." She heard a horse stamp in the next room. Honesty overcame her and she leaned toward him to confide, "If you want to know the truth, I thought Mr. Wilkes might be out here tinkering with your carriage to make it run faster . . . or redesigning the horses' reins so they would stop more quickly."

He smoked the cheroot, looked up at the cloud of smoke, and drawled, "I quiver to think of Mr. Wilkes touching my carriage."

She giggled. "I do, too. That was why I ran out here."

"I appreciate your concern."

Arabella hesitated before asking, "Are you terribly angry with me for bringing him?"

"We shall manage," he said in a forgiving voice.

"Yes." She huddled deeper into her pelisse.

He rose and put a hand down toward her. "You are cold. I should take you back to the house, so you can go back to bed and be rested for the morning."

"Are you feeling better?" she asked in a quiet voice.

Nodding, he put a strong arm around her shoulders and guided her back through a stableful of interested horses. Arabella and Lord Ridgeton crossed the lawn together in silence. At the back door, he turned to her and said simply, "Thank you."

She made no reply. None seemed necessary.

Sir William rode beside Lord Ridgeton the next morning as the carriage fell further and further behind them on a road lumpy with carriage tracks. The trees that had formed a leafy archway for the first mile had given way to open pastures. Here and there spots of white chalk showed through.

"I wish you could have stayed longer, Cedric."

"Miss Fairingdale would have had my head," the marquess said lightly.

Sir William snorted. "Since when are you afraid of a woman?"

"Since I met her."

"Hah."

Lord Ridgeton grinned. "She has bedeviled me the whole Season to go to Manchester. She finally got her way." When Arabella had first descended on him in his study, he had never thought he would look back on the moment and think it humorous. At the time, he had been annoyed and insulted. Now he saw that Arabella had simply been acting like Arabella.

"It isn't the worst punishment in the world to make a journey with a lovely young lady, you know." Sir William looked at him keenly. "She has very pretty eyes, by the by. They're as blue as the stained-glass window in our country church."

"I haven't noticed."

"Of course you've noticed, Cedric," Sir William said, contradicting him with a laugh. "I saw you glancing toward her last night. You look like a man who could be besotted with her if you let yourself. Why not let yourself? Is anything about her unacceptable?"

The marquess pulled on the reins when a hare darted across the road in front of him. "She's accepted by society, if that is what you mean. She has only limited funds." Arabella had declined his offer to buy her share of the mill, so her circumstances must not be too straited. As far as being besotted with her, that was out of the question. He and Arabella would cross swords at every turn. "She is a good woman, but certainly not the sort for me."

"Ah, well . . ."

Still, when he remembered their talk last night, he softened toward her. She might be headstrong and determined about the things she wanted, but she could also show a woman's tenderness.

She was still going to want her way about the mill, though, he reminded himself. He had come to like her better, but men were still the best judges of how business should be conducted. The mill was probably being handled properly.

He was mulling that thought over when Sir William took his leave and started back to Wilmingham Hall. Well, he would deal with the problem of the mill once they were in Manchester. For now, there was no reason to overset Arabella. Why not enjoy her company while he could?

Chapter 7

JUST BEFORE dark, they stopped for the night at the Hen and Hickory. The little inn of plaster and wood looked picture pretty outside. Once inside, though, Arabella saw that it was small and dark and crowded. The ceiling hung low like a dark, looming cloud.

The rooms were no better. Arabella and Emily were given two narrow beds in a room at the front of the house. The noise from the yard below proved overbearing, however, so Arabella found the innkeeper and asked to be moved.

Once settled in a room at the other end of the hall, Arabella bathed the road dust from her and changed into a sea green gown.

At dinnertime, she met Lord Ridgeton in the private parlor he had engaged for their meal. Emily did not accompany her. The companion had complained of stiffness, but Arabella knew the real reason was that Emily had still not mastered feeding herself gracefully. Arabella allowed Emily her vanity.

The meal was served by a smiling elderly woman at a small oval table. As the dishes were being placed, Arabella looked at the marquess across the bright candle tips and saw that his hair shone from a recent wash and his skin gleamed from a brisk washing.

"Are your rooms comfortable?" he asked.

"Yes. And yours, milord?"

"Our quarters are crowded. They had to bring a trundle bed into my room for my valet." He smiled sardonically. "Charles is already out of reason cross at having to sit up front all day when he thought he should have been inside the carriage. A trundle bed was the final insult. He is at this very moment trying to calm himself with some of the innkeeper's best spirits."

"Oh, dear." Shaking her head, she picked up her fork.

He gave an indifferent shrug. "Charles will recover."

Arabella had noticed the valet each time they stopped to change horses and at luncheon. He had strutted about the yard full of his own importance. "Do you worry about him sinking too far into his cups?" she asked.

"No. He will . . . er . . . find other diversions."

Women, of course. Arabella had not reached her advanced age without discovering that backstairs romances occurred.

"What of your companion?" he asked.

Did he think it improper for them to be alone together? Well, they had spent time in a deserted stable only last night. "Emily was tired. Traveling wearies her. She looks forward to returning to Kent and settling down for good."

"And you? Do you anticipate the calm and quiet of Kent?"

She hesitated. She had enjoyed the London Season far more than she had anticipated. What would it be like to settle back into her little house with no prospect of ever leaving it again? "It may not be as quiet as it was before since we have a new master at Baxter House. Lady Baxter seldom entertained, but Lord Seagraves intends to do more."

He gave her a sharp look over the rim of his brimming glass. "Lord Seagraves?"

She blinked. He did not have to bark at her. "Yes."

"I have seen him a time or two since his return. I knew him as a boy. I disliked him."

"Well, that was many years ago," she said briskly, annoyed at his judgment of a man she had come to like. "I find him perfectly charming."

Lord Ridgeton set the glass down without ever taking his gaze from her. "He was forced to go to America because of rumors he kept a houseful of young women servants. A man is allowed his appetites, but he must be discreet. The tales of how he conducted his household were scandalous."

"Goodness, I would think you had better things to do than listen to gossip." Arabella gave him a tough little smile that suggested if he could not be kind, he should forebear to speak at all. She felt particularly compelled to defend Lord Seagraves because he had worried about fitting back into English life. No wonder. He must have met with others who treated him as shabbily as Lord Ridgeton.

"Is he a friend of yours, Miss Fairingdale?" he asked coolly.

"I have met him on more than one occasion, and I daresay I shall see more of him in Kent." Of course she would see him in Kent. She lived on the man's property, but she was not going to tell Lord Ridgeton that.

"I would be careful to not let the friendship develop too deeply. It's said he left America amid rumors."

"Lord Ridgeton, I consider myself an excellent

judge of character. I assume your sources are wrong." Lady Hector had liked him well enough.

"Must you challenge every single thing I tell you?" he demanded irritably.

"If I think it is wrong, yes."

He gave her a final cool look, then turned to attack his food.

Conversation after that spiraled downward to short observations about the weather and clipped comments on the food. Lord Ridgeton might look resplendent in a coat of deep navy and a cravat tied with skill, but he was still arrogant and overbearing.

Arabella found it difficult to credit she and the marquess had enjoyed such a comfortable exchange in Sir William's stables. The marquess could be human, but he did not appear to be all the time.

Arabella was glad when the meal ended. She went back upstairs, opened her door, and entered a dark room. Quietly she closed the door and moved through the darkness so as not to disturb Emily. Her companion was sleeping so soundly Arabella did not even hear her breathing.

After fumbling with the buttons down her back, Arabella loosened the dress enough to slide out of it. Clad in her thin chemise, she crawled into bed. She hoped tomorrow was more pleasant than today had been. With that in her mind, she fell asleep.

Arabella awakened some time later to a piercing scream. She bolted upright just as another scream raked the darkness. Dear heavens, it sounded like Emily! But the screams were not coming from the other bed. They were coming from outside the room.

Arabella jumped up and wrapped the bedclothes around her as she ran to the door and wrenched it open. Outside in the hallway, a drowsy man and a worried woman looked up and down the narrow hallway.

"Did you hear screams?" Arabella demanded.

"Yes, from the room at the end of the hall."

Clutching at the bedclothes, she raced down the hall and pushed the door open. The marquess stood in a corner of the room holding a candle over Emily and speaking sternly to her. Charles sat on the edge of the trundle bed staring blearily down at the bare floor.

"Shut the door, Miss Fairingdale," Lord Ridgeton ordered.

She didn't react. She stood motionless, scanning faces and trying to determine what was happening. Or had happened.

Lord Ridgeton crossed the room in half a dozen long steps and slammed the door.

The noise startled Arabella into action. She rushed to Emily and wrapped her arms around her companion. "You're shaking. What's wrong? Are you injured?"

"I—I don't know."

Arabella kept her arms protectively fenced around Emily and turned to confront Lord Ridgeton. "What is the meaning of this? Was Emily lured here? Dragged here? Why wasn't she in her room?"

"Your companion was in Charles's bed and—"

"In his bed!" She whirled toward the blinking valet. "Pray, how did that occur?"

"I suppose she chose to be there," Charles mumbled, and blinked as if trying to fix his gaze.

"Of course she did not choose to be in your bed," Arabella shouted at him. "Miss Windell is a decent woman of impeccable morals, not fodder for your lust." She rounded on the marquess. "Where were you when this was taking place?"

"I was here."

"Didn't you attempt to protect her?"

"There was no reason to. It was clear that—"

"No reason!" Dear heavens, Emily couldn't even see. What sort of person was this valet? And why hadn't the marquess stopped him? Emily shook in her arms and Arabella patted her. "You needn't worry; no one will harm you now."

"Someone got into bed with me," she said in a trembling voice. Emily folded further into Arabella's arms. "This is dreadful. Please take me out of here."

"Of course." Arabella looked back at the marquess. "As soon as Emily is better, I wish to speak to you, milord," she said in killing accents.

"Miss Fairingdale, you are exaggerating what happened here. Miss Windell may be a bit frightened, but her virtue was not tarnished."

Arabella was not going to let him dismiss the incident so easily. She had a great deal to say to him. First, though, she must calm her companion. She led Emily from the room.

"I'm so mortified," her companion said as they moved slowly down the hallway.

"There is no need to be. It is Charles who behaved without conscience."

"You see, I—"

Ignoring the half dozen people who had gathered in the hall, Arabella opened her door and herded Emily inside. After guiding her to the bed and pushing her gently down onto it, Arabella sat down beside her.

"I know you are overset. We can return to London immediately if you wish," Arabella said in a soothing voice. "I do not expect you to travel with someone so lacking in decency as Lord Ridgeton's valet has shown himself to be." The marquess's own part remained unclear, and she intended to get an answer to that once Emily was reassured.

"No, you don't understand. The fault is mine. I went to sleep in his bed."

Arabella stared at her ashen face before asking carefully, "Intentionally?"

Emily jerked upright. "Certainly not! I believed I was in my own room. They had moved us from one room to another, you see, and I was tired and confused. At any rate, I heard someone come in later and get in the other bed, but I thought it was you. It must have been the marquess." She covered her face with her hands and her voice fell to a shamed whisper. "How lowering. I shall never be able to face either of them again."

A sharp rap sounded on the door. Lord Ridgeton, of course. She had a sinking feeling she had made some unwise accusations and she had no wish to face him at the moment.

The firm knock sounded again. "Open this door. I know perfectly well you are in there."

She didn't respond.

He muttered something not meant for delicate ears, then pounded on the door. It was plain he was not going to leave. Wrapping the cover securely around her, Arabella rose with a sigh, went to the door, and pulled it open. "Yes?"

He stepped into the room and shut the door behind him. "I hope you are pleased with yourself, Miss Fairingdale. You took a fragile situation and managed to make a royal mull of it."

She lifted her chin. "How was I to know Emily went to sleep in the wrong bed?"

"If you had listened before flying off like a wild bird, I would have explained everything. Then I would not be dealing with a valet foolishly trying to give me his notice."

Arabella tried to muster her defenses. "You are partly to blame. You insinuated Charles would find a companion for the night. I assumed he had found Emily."

"A *willing* companion. He would never force anyone. I can assure you he is far more overset than Miss Windell."

Looking at Emily's pale, tear-streaked face, Arabella doubted that.

The marquess also turned to Emily and addressed her in greatly softened accents: "I am sorry about this unfortunate incident, Miss Windell. I will do my best to make everything easier for you. If you wish to return to London, we shall do so. If you prefer that Charles be left behind to follow on the stage, I shall see to that, too."

"You are m-most kind."

"I know you are shaken. Try to sleep now and we can talk in the morning."

She nodded mutely.

Lord Ridgeton gave Arabella one final, searing look and was gone.

She gnawed at her lower lip. Oh, dear. It was a bad thing to lose his goodwill just when they were nearing Manchester. She would have to patch things up.

Lord Ridgeton was standing near the watering trough the next morning when Arabella stepped out of the inn. She looked slim and pretty in a pale blue gown as she tilted her head back to look up at the sky. She might look fetching, but she had created unnecessary turmoil last night and he was still seething.

He watched her cross the yard to where Charles stood next to the stable door. The marquess could not hear what she said, but she held the valet's gaze the whole time with her intent look. When she left, Charles was smiling.

What was the baggage up to? he wondered suspiciously as she approached him. In the bright daylight, she looked meek and humble. He was not fooled.

"I apologized to Charles," she said as she halted near the watering trough. She paused.

If she was waiting for him to encourage her, she would catch cold. He stood impassively, one hand in his pocket, the other hooked over the top rail of a gate.

Arabella took a deep breath and continued, "I also owe you an apology for last night. I was too hasty to form an opinion." She cleared her throat and looked uncertainly down at her hands. "I hope you will forgive me. It was wrong of me to make accusations without first discovering what had happened."

"You *were* wrong," he agreed coldly. "You insulted both Charles and me. Didn't you realize I would never allow anyone to harm your companion? Or you. Surely you have that much faith in me."

She continued to look at her hands, her long lashes fanned downward like tiny feathers.

"No, apparently you do not have any faith in me," he said brusquely. She would not listen to him or to anyone. She might seem contrite today, but she had raged at him like a warrior queen last night. He could still see her with the covers flung over her—looking at him with blazing blue eyes. If he had not been so angry, he might have thought her magnificent.

"I know this is difficult for you to understand, but I have been accustomed to caring for myself and

Emily," she said slowly. "It was my natural instinct to do so last night."

That gave him pause, but he refused to soften completely.

A horse clomped up to the watering trough. The marquess glanced at his own horses enjoying their oats in the pasture beside the stables. They would have the day to enjoy the field, because he had decided they would not leave today. "We shall remain here until tomorrow," he told Arabella shortly.

"Whatever you wish."

At least she had the good sense not to oppose him on this. Nodding abruptly he pivoted on the toe of his boot and left her behind.

Charles trailed him back into the inn and up to their cramped room. He cleared his throat twice before venturing, "I don't wish to interfere, milord, but Miss Fairingdale did apologize."

"That was no more than she should have done," Lord Ridgeton answered curtly.

"Begging your pardon, milord, but I've never known a lady of Quality to apologize even when she was wrong."

"Miss Fairingdale should not have been wrong in the first place." Even to the marquess's own ears, it was a pompous, ridiculous statement. "Besides, I am doing enough for her by taking her to Manchester," he muttered.

Charles said nothing.

Devil take it. He did not have to mollify Charles or anyone else. He was in the right and would not be made to feel he was being unreasonable.

What he needed was a fast, reckless ride away from this crowded little inn. It would give him the chance to clear his mind of Arabella Fairingdale and of last night's events.

"Prepare my riding clothes," he commanded.

"Yes, milord," Charles said, without inflection.

A short time later, Lord Ridgeton left the room wearing a dun-colored coat and dark riding breeches. He swatted his crop carelessly against his leg as he stalked to the stables. There he charged a stablehand with saddling his horse. When the mane-tossing bay was ready, the marquess sauntered off down the lane. The vines and flowers crowding up against the packed-dirt lane made speed impossible. Once he reached the open road, however, he intended to give the horse its head.

Meanwhile, he pondered darkly that he should never have left London. The Season might have bored him, but at least he had not been obliged to deal with the wounded feelings of servants or with Arabella on a daily basis. Not that she had been wholly unpleasant. There had been moments when he had enjoyed her company thoroughly. Her voice was soft and purling when she read to Emily from the guidebook—and she had been sweetly considerate the night she had come to him at Sir William's stables. Those memories helped cloud out some of his anger toward her regarding last night.

He rounded a corner and saw Arabella standing by the side of the road. A basket of flowers swung from her arm. She wore a calico dress and a light shawl dripped off her shoulders. Her cheeks were as pink as the posies sticking out of her basket.

It was hard to be angry when she looked so fetching. He pulled the horse to a stop. "Hello, Arabella."

"Hello," she said tentatively.

There was a moment of silence between them.

"I took the path here from the inn." She gestured over her shoulder toward a narrow path. "I thought flowers would cheer Emily. She can't see them, but she likes the smell and the touch." Arabella plucked another flower and cast a timid, sidelong glance at him.

He couldn't repress a smile at seeing her so uncharacteristically meek. "Do you think Miss Windell will be recovered enough to travel by tomorrow?"

"I daresay she will." Sighing, Arabella pulled a shaggy leaf from a stem. "It is Emily's dignity that is damaged the most. She is embarrassed to see you or Charles again."

"Tell her she needn't be," he said quietly.

She nodded. The fringe of her shawl flitted about in the wind and her hair played around her face. Yes, she was fetching. The marquess slid to the ground and let the horse crop grass beside the road.

"Perhaps I should take some flowers to Charles," he said, with a dry laugh. "He is out of humor with me."

"Oh? I thought he seemed pleased after I spoke with him this morning."

"He is entirely in charity with you, but he thinks I am being too harsh with you."

She made no reply.

The marquess picked a flower and turned the subject away from him. "I have not seen Mr. Wilkes this morning."

She laughed and glanced at him. Her eyes looked even bluer under the azure sky. "Are you afraid of what he may do with a day of idle time?"

"I did wonder," he said drily. He let the horse continue to eat; he had the whole day in which to take a ride.

Arabella pulled the dancing shawl more firmly up onto her shoulders. "He's really quite brilliant. It's a pity none of his inventions have flourished. Papa was like that. He tried and tried but never succeeded."

"Did you live with your father after your mother died?" he asked. Arabella had said her mother had died when she was nine—a tender age at which to lose a mother. Perhaps it explained why she was so independent.

"For a few years. We moved about a great deal. Papa was very learned," she said earnestly. "We would settle down for a time while he taught at a university. Once he taught Latin to some unruly boys in a public school." She smiled at the memory.

"Surely that is not the life for a young lady. What of your education?"

The basket swung from her arm as she returned to picking flowers. "That is what Mama's friends said. They were shocked to discover Papa was teaching me himself in the evenings. When I was twelve, they determined it was time for me to be properly finished."

He tried to imagine Arabella as an unformed girl. He saw her with straight corn silk hair and skin rosy from the sun, and, of course, those rich blue eyes. The boys at the public school had surely daydreamed of her.

"Several women came to speak to Papa," she continued. "They were very kind to me, but I heard them talking to Papa when I was supposed to be sleeping. They said Mama would want me to have all the advantages of a good education. So I went away to school and learned to draw and play the pianoforte, but it was not nearly so interesting as when Papa taught me to shoe a horse."

He arched one eyebrow in astonishment. "Shoe a horse?"

Arabella giggled and put a flower in the basket. "I wasn't very good at it—and I daresay I couldn't do it now—but it was more entertaining than sitting with a roomful of girls who talked only of their prospects for a good marriage."

"Indeed." Especially since her own prospects had not been good. He wondered if the kindly ladies who had intervened on her behalf had considered that Arabella would learn accomplishments she would never use. In her position, there had never been any prospects of a brilliant match.

Arabella peered down into the basket. "Do you think these are enough flowers?"

He thought it quite enough, but he was reluctant to end their talk. "Maybe you should pluck a few more."

She agreeably turned back to picking flowers. Just then the breeze caught her shawl and dragged one end to the ground. He bent to pick it up at the same time she did, and the basket of flowers spilled to the ground. Petals and stems and leaves lay in a heap on the road.

"Drat," she mumbled, and bent to retrieve them.

He knelt beside her, not caring that the knees of his trousers were being dirtied. "Never mind," he said, trying to console her, and scooped up a handful of flowers. "Emily can't see them, and they are still as fragrant and feel as soft as before."

"I suppose so." Still, Arabella looked disappointed.

His fingers grazed hers as she reached for the flowers. She gave him a quick smile and continued her task. When the basket was full, they both rose.

She looked up at him, and he saw soft red lips and a pair of pretty blue eyes. Yes, he could well imagine her father's students fantasizing about her. Even he, a man of experience, saw much in her to tempt. He had sampled her lips once and found them wholly satisfying. What if he were to kiss her again as soundly? Would she draw back . . . or would she melt against him again?

He was considering whether to try when the sound of hoofbeats interrupted. He stepped quickly away, pushing back irrational thoughts brought on by sunlight and flowers and quiet lanes. He might no longer be angry with her, but he must maintain a proper distance.

For him to do otherwise with an unprotected woman would be to act as a coxcomb.

Over the following days, the party traversed the dry, sunny grassland of the midlands and followed the road beneath tall elms and strong beeches and oaks. Each time the landscape began to look too much the same, Arabella would spy a ruined castle atop some windswept hilltop or see a lavish mansion surrounded by parkland.

She enjoyed the passing scenery, but she was also anxious to reach Manchester. Still, during the course of sitting across from the marquess, a comfortableness had grown between them. They played cards occasionally and sometimes he read to her from the guidebook. He talked a little about his family and she told him more about hers.

She knew him better by the time they pulled into the brick-lined drive of the White Willow in Manchester. The inn was an old Tudor mansion with rows of pointed-arch windows and a series of pitched roofs piggybacking atop one another.

They reached the inn late in the afternoon and by nightfall Arabella was ensconced in a sitting room adjoining her spacious bedchamber. She brushed her hair in the lamplight and savored the satisfaction of knowing tomorrow the marquess would see to Harry's release. Then Lord Ridgeton would be free to devote himself to the far more important concern of the mill.

Closing her eyes, Arabella slid the brush through her hair. The soft bristles tingled and warmed her scalp. What a nice, calm sleep she meant to enjoy tonight. After endless hours in the carriage and too many nights spent on lumpy mattresses, she could relax at last.

"Are you all right, Arabella?" Emily asked.

"Yes, why do you ask?"

"You've sighed twice in the space of two minutes."

Arabella opened her eyes and smiled. "That's because I am happy. We are in Manchester, and soon we shall see results at the mill. All we need is Lord Ridgeton's money."

"Do you think he will give it?" Emily asked doubtfully.

"Yes." Arabella resumed brushing her hair. "At first I thought he was a selfish person, but I see he has a gentler, hidden side. He will do what is right." To falter in that confidence would be to betray herself and the workers.

"I've come to like the marquess very much," Emily said. "He is attentive to you and quite kind to me. He always keeps a firm hand on my arm when we go into and out of the inns. He has strong hands," she added.

Arabella had noticed his hands herself but forebore to say so. She had noticed a number of other things about him, from the fact his fingers were blunt-tipped to the way he cocked his head to one side when in thought. She had seen his face when it was a stern mask and when it was alight with laughter. She had noted that his teeth were white and strong and that his face had the smallest dimple on one side. She had had a lot of time to study his countenance during the drive and had decided she liked it quite a lot.

Emily rose. "It has been a long day and I am exhausted. I must retire for the evening." She disappeared through a door leading off one side of the sitting room.

Retiring sounded like a good idea, Arabella decided, and entered her own bedchamber through a door in the opposite wall. She undressed quickly and sank onto the large bed.

She was soon asleep.

Arabella awoke much later and struggled uneasily against a tangle of bedclothes. Who was shouting? And what was that smell? Pushing herself up on her elbows, she sniffed the air. Something was on fire.

Dear lord! Jumping up, she ran to the window and pushed back the draperies. There she saw an orange glow illuminating the night sky.

Arabella grabbed her pelisse and a taper and rushed out the door and down the steps. A crowd had already gathered on the street in front of the inn.

Judging from the growing brightness of the sky, the fire was spreading rapidly. She bit back a groan at the thought that those burning buildings might house sleeping children or old, frail people. Were men and women fighting to escape even as she stood here? She clutched her pelisse tighter around her and offered silent prayers.

Some men pushed by her, heading in the direction of the fire. Others stayed rooted to the street and watched in fascination and horror. From somewhere in the distance she heard her name, but she was too intent on watching the flames to look around.

"Arabella!" Strong hands gripped her and turned her. She blinked up into Lord Ridgeton's face.

"What the devil are you doing out here?" He was fully dressed, she noted absently, except for a cravat. "God's teeth, woman, you don't even have shoes on."

She had not noticed the cold cobblestones until now.

"You should not be outside by yourself," he said sharply.

"There is a fire." She gestured in the direction of the blaze.

"I know that," he said impatiently, "but that does not change the fact you should not be out here alone. Come back inside this moment."

She could accomplish nothing here anyway, so she allowed him to lead her upstairs to her door.

"Go inside and remain there," he directed, and swung back toward the stairs.

She caught his sleeve, clutching at the smooth fabric of his coat. "Where are you going?"

"To help fight the blaze."

Her grip tightened until her fingers dug past the material and into flesh. "You can't go. It isn't safe."

He pried her fingers off his arm and said with quiet firmness, "Arabella, the fire will continue to spread unless some effort is made to control it. The only way to accomplish that is for enough men to fight it."

Knowing he was right did not prevent Arabella from being afraid for him. She scanned his face and saw a faint line across his cheek where his face had lain pressed into the pillow not long before. The mark made him seem softer and more human. "You will be careful, won't you?" she asked in a small voice.

"Of course."

"I—" She ground to a halt, unsure what she meant to say.

"Yes, Arabella?" His eyes were shining pieces of jet in the murky hallway.

Giving in to impulse, she reached up and touched his hair lightly. The dark strands felt thick and unruly beneath her fingers. She wanted to burrow her fingers in deeper, but reason made her pull her hand reluctantly back.

"Go to your room, Arabella," he said gently.

He was gone, disappearing down the dark hallway. Arabella stood in the empty hall for a long time fighting back tears. Finally she turned and went into her sitting room.

Emily stood by the window. She looked up with a start. "Arabella? Is that you?"

"Yes."

"Where have you been?" she asked, with concern. "I thought you were asleep."

"I was outside watching the fire." And in the hall watching the marquess go off to face danger. What if something happened to him?

"The fire is quite large, isn't it? I can tell that the whole sky is aglow."

"It must be several buildings. Lord Ridgeton has gone to help fight it." She stopped just before her voice cracked.

Arabella and Emily stood in silence.

"I won't be able to sleep if I go to bed," Emily said.

Arabella knew she would not sleep, either.

"He has been in battle, so he knows how to be careful," Emily said after a few minutes.

Arabella knew her words were meant to calm and reassure her. "Of course he will be careful," she agreed, with spirit. "He will not die here in his own country after living through the campaigns abroad."

"Is your voice trembling?"

"Only because my feet are chilled." It wasn't her feet but her heart that was chilled at the possibility of something terrible befalling Lord Ridgeton. Fighting fires was dangerous. She had once seen a church burn and had watched in horror as bricks fell and killed a man.

Nervously she pleated the fabric of her chemise with restless fingers. It threatened to be a very long night.

Chapter 8

LORD RIDGETON arrived at the fire to find dozens already battling valiantly. He joined two men at an engine the size of a small carriage that had pumping brakes attached on either end. The men labored to keep a stream of water jetting against the nearest building.

The fragile wood structures yielded easily to the onslaught of the fire. He saw embers leaping from building to building. Burning chunks of wood splattered out into the roads, taunting those trying to mount a defense.

He fought back his dismay and began pushing the heavy handle of the pump up and down, up and down. A hook and ladder truck raced up nearby and behind it steamed another fire engine. The engine began shooting water in their direction, and it was not long before he stood drenched from the spray shooting off the hoses.

"Lucky it's mills and no one is inside at night," the man on the other side of the pump said.

"Could have been in the daytime," the one handling the hose replied. "That would have meant a lot of lives lost."

Lord Ridgeton pushed down harder on the metal rod controlling the water and felt blisters rise on his palms. He kept pumping.

"If it had been daytime, the doors would have

been locked to keep the blokes inside," the man across from the marquess shouted over the roar of the blaze.

"Bodies," the other grunted as the water pulsed and spewed erratically from the hose. "There would have been a lot of bodies."

The marquess concentrated on his task and tried not to think that one of these buildings might be his own. Were the doors locked inside his mill in the daytime? He watched flames strip exterior walls from two- and three-story structures to reveal warren's wrens of tiny rooms and narrow passages. Anyone inside would have soon been trapped.

Arabella had warned him about a fire in the mill. He had ignored her warnings and told her to leave such matters to those best equipped to deal with them. Even after he reached Manchester, he had intended to continue to ignore her. Oh, he would have pacified her by touring the factory, but he had not really intended to make changes.

With a grunt, he bore down harder on the pump. The trouble was he had not expected her to be right. After all, the men who ran the mills had been doing so for years. He had assumed they knew their business. It belatedly occurred to him those men were motivated by profit. If putting workers in danger meant extra money, it appeared many owners were willing to put their workers in peril.

He felt a flush of anger come over him as he continued working to fight the blaze. The owners had no right to put others in danger. The realization he had been one of those callous owners did not make him feel any better. He could not think about that now, he told himself, and continued pumping with an energy strengthened by guilt.

He worked without relief until he glanced toward

the sky some time later and saw morning pinking through.

"Watch it!"

Instinctively he threw up his hands and jumped backward. A flaming wall fell outward and struck the ground near him with a fierce hiss. Embers rained outward. Damn! This was as dangerous as the war.

The marquess helped pull the engine backward and returned to the pump. He was dripping water and coated with wet soot. He was also cold and tired, which might have explained why he became careless. At any rate, he reached down to move a timber in the path of the engine and felt pain rush up his hands. The log was sizzling hot. He jerked backward and held up his scorched hands.

A big man rushed over to him. "Did you burn yourself?"

Lord Ridgeton gave a stunned nod and continued to hold his hands outstretched.

The man looked at his palms. "You burned 'em good. You'll feel that tomorrow."

"I daresay I will," he said in a hollow voice. At the moment, a merciful numbness was spreading over his fingers and palms.

"Go home," the man urged gently.

"I can help a bit longer." He had seen men in battle who were far more seriously injured than he continue to fight.

"And do yourself more harm?" The man made a shooing motion with his hands. "Be gone with you. You're dead on your feet."

Nodding in resignation, the marquess started back to the inn with slightly unsteady steps.

Arabella saw the tired, bent form of the marquess through the window. His clothes were blackened and he had a large bloody gash on his arm.

He seemed to be forcing himself to take each step forward.

Biting her lip, she stifled a cry.

She ran downstairs and threw open the door just as he reached for the handle. They looked at each other in silence. She had never thought to see the well-groomed marquess reeking of smoke, his expensive clothes tattered and singed. He looked haggard and his damp hair clung to his scalp in wet patches. He would have been the talk of London if anyone from the ton had seen him. Arabella thought he had never looked more wonderful or more honorable.

She stretched out a hand toward him.

He shook his head. "Don't. You'll soil your gown."

Ignoring her yellow muslin day dress, she put her hand on his arm. "The frock doesn't signify. Are you hurt?"

"A few scratches."

It looked far worse, but she did not argue as they mounted the steps to the second floor.

"Charles will be devastated," he noted wrily. "I've ruined a perfectly good coat. Luckily I wasn't wearing a cravat."

She smiled for his sake. "Charles will recover." She did not like the drawn look of the marquess's face or the way his eyes were crinkled at the edges as if he were in pain. She slipped her arm around his waist and he did not resist as she assisted him up the steps.

His body felt firm and taut beneath her arm, but he moved with slow steps.

He hesitated at the door of his room. It was then she noticed how carefully he held his hands at his sides. Already dreading what she would see, Arabella picked up his left wrist and turned his hand palm up. She caught her breath at the sight of a red mass of blisters.

"What happened?" she asked in horror.

"I was careless and put my hands where I should not."

"Does it hurt fearfully?"

"Not so much."

He was lying. It even hurt her to look at the welts and bladders on his palms.

Just then the door opened and Charles appeared. He froze in disbelief. "My lord!"

The marquess managed a weak grin. "Yes, Charles. I know I look the worse for wear, but I'm right as a trivet. Or will be as soon as I have a large glass of something strong."

"Of course, my lord." Charles was already hovering beside his master and leading him into the room.

Arabella knew her presence was no longer necessary. In fact, the two men stood waiting for her to leave, so the valet could peel the blackened clothes from his master and help him climb into a tub of warm water. Of course she could not be present for those ablutions, but still she lingered.

"You look tired, Arabella. Why don't you go rest?" Lord Ridgeton suggested. His words were thin and he looked ready to collapse.

Charles added his own dismissal, with a curt, "I shall care for His Lordship."

"Yes, of course. If there is anything I can do . . ." She broke off guiltily. The marquess looked so miserable that she longed to comfort him. Making it all worse was the knowledge she was partly to blame. If she had not insisted he come to Manchester, this would never have happened.

"I shall tend to everything," Charles intoned firmly, and shut the door in her face.

The memory of the marquess's raw, scalded hands galvanized her into action. Arabella was no authority on the treatment of wounds, but the mistress of the house would know what to do.

She rushed down the narrow back stairs to the kitchen. In her haste, she almost fell off the bottom step. Mrs. Anglesbury, a doughy woman with a brisk manner, looked up from a table where she sat working on menus.

"I need your help," Arabella blurted. "Lord Ridgeton's hands are burned."

"Goodness." The stout woman rose immediately and went to a long cupboard near the back door. "How badly?"

"I cannot say. Fierce-looking blisters have already formed."

The older woman began laying out supplies. "Here, you can help me."

Arabella was glad to cut a piece of lint and began mixing lime water and linseed oil. She worked quickly, spilling some of the liquid in her haste, but spurred by the knowledge Lord Ridgeton was in pain.

"Take this up to him," Mrs. Anglesbury directed when she had a tray prepared.

Arabella returned to Lord Ridgeton's room holding the cloth-covered tray carefully in front of her. Charles answered her knock. "I have brought something for Lord Ridgeton," she said.

The valet looked distrustfully from her to the tray. "To eat? He already has food."

"This is to apply to his wounds."

"I have applied flour."

She brushed past him. "I have brought something better."

The marquess was sitting in a dressing gown in a chair facing out the window. When he turned toward her, her heart lurched. The soot had been cleaned from his face, but he still looked disheveled and drawn.

She tightened her grip on the tray. "I have brought you something to ease the pain, milord." She crossed the room and set the tray beside him. "Let me see your hands."

He folded them closer to his body and informed her, "Charles has already attended to me."

"I know he has," she explained, "but I am going to do a better job."

Behind her, she heard the valet exhale a trembling, indignant breath.

Arabella reached for Lord Ridgeton's hands; he reluctantly spread them out. White flour fell from his hands onto her dress. She paid no mind to that as she began applying a warm poultice.

"After a few days, we shall dress the wound with Turner's cerate," she said in comforting tones. She felt him wince and looked quickly up to his face. His eyes looked dull with pain. "I have brought paregoric to relieve your suffering."

The marquess scowled. "I'll not take opium. It's for fainting misses and old women."

"It is for anyone in pain," Arabella said reasonably.

She got back a cool, stubborn look. "I do not want it."

"Please, don't make me argue with you. I bear some of the responsibility for your burns and I am going to help you whether you wish it or not."

"I shall be fine with a little rest," he grumbled. "All this fussing will only make me worse."

She pursed her lips and remained where she was. "The poultice will help your hands. If you won't take the opium, at least try the drink I have brought."

"What is in it?"

"Cream of tartar and a little lime juice in warm water."

He pulled a face.

Oblivious to his dislike, Arabella brought the cup to his lips. "Take just one sip."

He swallowed.

"Good." She rewarded him with a smile. He looked like an unhappy child who should be put to bed and coddled. Arabella felt a surprisingly strong desire to nurture him. She wanted to pull the cover closer around his shoulders and put his feet up on a stool.

"He is tired and should rest now," Charles announced stiffly from behind her.

"You are right." She rose slowly. "I shall return later."

Neither man replied.

Undeterred by their lack of enthusiasm, she returned to the marquess's chamber three hours later. Charles let her in. She glided past him to where Lord Ridgeton sat in the same chair.

His color looked better—but his lowered brow suggested his temper was worse.

"How are you feeling?" she asked lightly.

"Fine." He gave her a cursory glance, then turned to stare into the fire.

Uninvited, she sat down. "Have you eaten?"

"No, he has not," Charles said from behind her.

Arabella looked at a large silver tray beside Lord Ridgeton, where the food sat growing cold. "Surely you are hungry, milord."

"I believe he is," Charles interjected.

Lord Ridgeton gave his valet a hard look before sweeping a look across Arabella that was no softer.

She glanced at his lordship's red, swollen hands

and realized it would hurt to curve his fingers around a fork or touch a knife.

She had a solution.

Turning to Charles, she said, "I shall attend to Lord Ridgeton. You may leave now." When he did not, she rose and escorted him to the door. Ignoring his mutinous looks, she pushed him out the door and shut it. Then she swung back toward the marquess and smiled.

He watched her warily as she approached.

"The carrots look good," she said. She sat back down and pulled the chair close to him. Then she scooped carrots onto the fork and brought the offering to his mouth.

He stared at her. "What are you doing?"

"I'm feeding you."

"No, you are not." He clamped his mouth into a defiant line. "No one has fed me since I was in leading strings, and no one is going to now."

For all his resistance, she thought he looked with longing at the fork. "Let me taste them for you." She ate some carrots and pronounced, "Quite good. Nicely seasoned." She took another bite.

He glared at her. "Are you going to eat my food?"

"Well, you don't want it, do you?"

He looked at her a long, considering moment. His hair was still damp from a bath and his skin was pink and sootless. "Sometimes I don't know whether to turn you over my lap and spank you or laugh at your willfulness."

"Spanking me would make your hands hurt even more," she pointed out calmly. It would also put her in a most indelicate position. She brushed aside the inappropriate image his words conjured up.

"Yes, but it might give me a great deal of satisfaction," he grumbled.

"Eating will give you more satisfaction and will help build your strength." She offered him a bite of strawberry jam. After a long, stubborn moment, he opened his mouth and ate it. Progress. She brought a second sample forward and her knuckles brushed his lips as she inserted the fork into his mouth. The touch of his mouth against her skin felt intimate and unnecessarily pleasant. She hesitated.

"Are you going to give me another bite or do you intend to let me starve?"

Arabella pushed a mouthful of stew toward him. He ate obediently. She dipped the spoon back into the stew, inserted it in his mouth, and watched him chew. His brown eyes never left her face.

The quiet between them was broken only by the clattering of silverware. He was eating, but he was also watching her closely enough to take the edge off her briskness. Arabella was irrelevantly aware she had not combed her hair. It must look a mess. The yellow muslin was no longer fresh, either. She ran a hand down her gown and looked back to see him watching her steadily.

"Would you like a drink of water?" she asked quickly, and spilled some of it when she reached for the glass.

"Does it make you uncomfortable when I look at you, Arabella?" he asked.

"No. Well . . . perhaps a bit." She busied herself flicking drops of water from her gown.

"Why?"

"I don't know." She must attend to the business of feeding him and forget the nuances and undercurrents between them, she cautioned herself.

He ate several more bites before asking, "Would you put out the candle across the room? It is far too bright."

Arabella did not find the candle too bright, but

she extinguished it anyway and returned to her chair. The softer light shaded his face in pale blues and grays.

"That's better." He continued watching her with those unfathomable dark eyes. "Do you know I wanted to kiss you the other day on the lane?"

A pulse fluttered at the base of her throat. She did not answer.

"You looked so pretty I could not help myself. You look pretty now—soft and luminous."

Arabella put down the spoon and sat motionless.

The marquess brought his damaged hands up to her face and pulled her gently toward him. She felt the wet blisters against her cheeks—and she leaned toward him because to resist would hurt his hands. Or at least that was part of the reason she bent toward him.

She and the marquess were within inches of each other. When she looked into his eyes, she saw the same boldness she had noted in Peterby's. But there was more here. Lord Ridgeton's gaze was masculine and knowing, but it was also full of longing. Or maybe she recognized her own longing clotting up inside her and threatening to choke off her breathing. She and the marquess remained exactly where they were until the waiting seemed unbearable. Finally he bent toward her and her lashes fluttered closed.

She also sighed with relief when his breath skimmed down her throat. Then his lips touched hers. His first kisses were light, darting strokes that were too delicate to stir her deeply but strong enough to make her thirst for more. Then his mouth curved purposefully over hers and she felt the moist, sensual edge of his lips encompassing hers. His deepening kiss awakened velvet longings within her. Arabella was amazed that a small amount of pressure from his lips could make her dazed, tantalized, and yielding.

Pictures spun before her closed eyes. She saw him standing tall and fire-blackened. She saw him in riding clothes looking at her with soft humor. She saw him striding into a room and filling it with his presence. Suddenly all the images faded into a red blur, and the power of his kiss turned her limbs leaden. His lips ran riot across hers; she wanted the intensity and the feeling to last forever.

What was left of her reason told her she must not lose herself in his embrace. She should pull away from the warming caress of his lips and flee from the passion rising inside herself.

Arabella did neither. Instead she parted her lips. The touch of his tongue brushing across the interior of her mouth sent a jolt through her that was powerful enough to startle her back to reality.

She pulled away and looked into his heat-sated eyes. There she saw a mirror of her own desires, blurred emotions, and confusion.

Arabella had to get away and think clearly. "I shall send your valet in," she blurted. Rising in a swirl of skirts, she left the room.

She felt his gaze follow her every step of the way.

Lord Ridgeton watched the door close behind Arabella and sank back into the gold damask chair.

Even as his mind cleared, his body remained full of unchaste thoughts and smoldering desires. The fervor of her response had startled him. When a woman with gentle curves and a willowy waist offered her lips with such enticement, he could not but taste the wares. Rather than satisfying him, however, her kisses had only awakened further wants.

With a look down at his red and blistered hands,

he shook his head. What had he been thinking? Arabella was a lady—and his intentions toward her had been far from honorable. Her soft flesh and flaring hips and woman's bosom pressing against his body had generated a number of thoughts and desires—none of them pure.

Well, there was nothing to be done for it but to apologize to Arabella and make sure this did not happen again. However much she might stir his masculine desire, they would never suit. When they were together, tempers often flared and personalities clashed.

Added to that, he had already determined to wed a young debutante. In light of that, his actions were even more reprehensible.

As he pushed himself forward in the chair, he recalled his visit to Layton and his amazement that the crippled man had found purpose in life when the marquess could find none. Lord Ridgeton's lips twisted ironically as he realized Arabella had stirred him out of indifference. But he was expressing his newfound interest in life in all the wrong ways and places. He must transfer this passion elsewhere.

Lord Ridgeton levered himself out of the chair and moved to the bed. With luck, a brief sleep would clear his head.

He awoke an hour later to a gentle knock. Charles entered the room. His face bore a look of fastidious revulsion, and he dangled two odd-looking dark objects from his fingertips.

The marquess sat up on the side of the bed, taking care not to press down against the bedding with his hands. "What the devil are those?"

Charles cleared his throat. "Miss Fairingdale's coachman, Mr. Wilkes, fashioned these for you. They are gloves."

Lord Ridgeton stared at the bulky, misshapen objects. "Not like any gloves I've ever seen. If they are for me, I have no intention of wearing them."

Charles nodded. "I told Miss Fairingdale I doubted you would wish to wear them. She sent a message." He colored slightly.

Lord Ridgeton waited. "Well?"

"Miss Fairingdale said, 'Tell His Lordship not to be stubbornly vain. These will help save his hands from further injury.' "

The sharp-tongued vixen.

"The gloves," Charles explained, and placed them on a table as if they were stunned eels that might spring back to life, "are constructed of cotton inside and oilskin outside. These little caps near the cuffs are covers for holes. Water can be poured in to cushion your hands." He hesitated. "When the gloves are filled with water, I am given to understand they become quite large."

"Humph."

"Indeed. I shall tell Miss Fairingdale you said so."

"Do." Meddling woman. What did she think she was about kissing him with such abandon and then sending him messages as if he were a witless child? If there was one thing he disliked, it was an unpredictable woman. Never mind that she had decided, as he had, that their kisses should not have happened.

"Very good, milord. Is there anything else you wish?"

"No." As the valet started to leave, Lord Ridgeton amended, "Be here early tomorrow morning. I intend to go out."

Charles looked stricken. "So soon?"

"Yes. And extend my apologies to Miss Fairingdale that I shall not be able to dine with her." One meal fed from her hands was enough. He did not need her bending over him, or feeding him, or touching him. He most assuredly did not need to kiss her again.

That night Lord Ridgeton ate a solitary meal in his room, managing to feed himself. As he lingered over a dessert of gooseberry tart, he considered how best to apologize to Arabella. The easiest course would be to write her a note, but his hands hurt too much to hold a pen. It would be unthinkable for Charles to pen such a personal letter. Sighing, Lord Ridgeton decided he had no choice but to speak to Arabella in person.

He might as well be done with it. Pushing aside the unfinished dessert, he sent word for her to join him.

Arabella entered his sitting room a few minutes later. She wore a simple green gown with little figures on it and her hair curled girlishly. She might have been uncomfortable, but she was self-possessed enough to hide it. She smiled pleasantly and asked, "Are you feeling better?"

"Yes, yes." He swept her question aside and gestured impatiently toward a chair across from his at the fireplace. He wanted to get this over with as quickly as possible. "Pray sit down."

She did, folding her hands together and watching him with interest. He had ordered dozens of candles lit to prevent the room from looking even remotely romantic. Unfortunately the blazing candles gave Arabella's pale skin an opalescent sheen and her eyes sparkled a charming sapphire blue.

Brusquely he cleared his throat. "I wish to extend my deepest apologies for taking liberties with you, Miss Fairingdale. I assure you it will not happen again."

She nodded quietly. After a moment, she said, "I

must be honest and admit you were not solely to blame."

It was not the response he had expected. Why couldn't the woman lower her eyes and accept his apology with demure grace? He pressed on with strained gallantry: "I may not have forced kisses upon you, but it is always the gentleman's responsibility to protect a woman's virtue."

Arabella looked at him as if trying to read behind his words. "I do not hold you responsible, but if it makes you feel easier to apologize, then I accept."

In the light from the candles, her hair gleamed golden and her mouth looked soft and warm. "You have my assurance you are safe from any further untoward advances," he concluded firmly. "You need not fear me."

"I was never afraid of you," she said softly. "I knew you would not attempt anything without my consent. Even though a gentleman is bound by certain rules, sometimes he is swept away by his emotions."

He glared at her. "Arabella, a man and woman have no business letting their emotions run free. The more powerful and compelling those emotions, the more they must be held in check."

"It's true that certain boundaries must not be crossed, but we did not cross them."

Oh, but he had in his mind. Even now his thoughts wandered into pleasures far beyond kissing. Lord Ridgeton wrapped his hands around the arms of the chair and felt a jolt of pain that brought him back to sanity. "I am trying to act as a gentleman," he told her waspishly. "It is better for both of us if we forget what occurred."

"That would be difficult," she murmured.

"Then let us *pretend*," he said sharply, and could not help adding, "any other woman would have blushed and stammered and accepted my apology without argument."

Her head came up and a feisty glint invaded her eyes. "I am not any other woman, milord."

No, she was not. She was uniquely Arabella—lovely and maddening and honest to a fault. She looked enchanting with all the lights playing off her and her head held up high. Damn the extra candles.

He let a few moments pass. Then, in a distantly cordial voice, he inquired, "Have you and Miss Windell been keeping yourselves occupied?"

"We have walked about some," she replied in a tone to match his own.

"My carriage and driver are at your disposal if you should wish to drive outside the city to see the countryside."

"Thank you."

As he talked of inconsequential things, he thought about her admission she had wanted to kiss him. If she could show such beguiling passion in a kiss, what would she be like when giving herself totally? Lord Ridgeton pressed his hands hard against the chair arms again and the pain sobered him.

"Are you hurting?" she asked quickly.

"No, I am only tired."

She picked up her skirts and rose. "I shall leave you to rest."

"Thank you for coming to see me," he said formally.

He went to bed shortly after she left, but he did not fall asleep for a long time. He would have been better served to have sent a note, he decided. He should have known Arabella could not be depended upon to act meek and demure.

Chapter 9

"Is His Lordship feeling better?" Emily inquired when Arabella returned to the sitting room.

"He is feeling guilty." She did not know whether to be amused or insulted that he acted as if she had been an unwilling victim of his passion. She was not such a simpering miss as to endure an embrace she did not want. If it had been wrong, then they had both been wrong.

"Guilty?" Emily looked up from a teacup and Arabella realized her companion was practicing eating alone. "Whatever for?"

Arabella sighed. "It is a long story."

Emily did not press.

Sitting down across from her companion, Arabella let her head fall back against the high back of the chair as she thought of those moments in the marquess's arms. His apology had not held the weight of his kisses. She had discovered that she liked kissing him very much. It appeared, she acknowledged with the truth she always demanded of herself, that she had developed a *tendre* for Lord Ridgeton.

What was she to do about that? Lord Ridgeton had not acknowledged any feelings toward her. Perhaps he did not have any. His kisses could have been nothing more than a masculine need for conquest. When they had spoken moments ago he had given no indication of any more tender feelings.

"Did he mention Mr. Bartley?" Emily picked up her cup, took a careful sip, and slowly worked to place the cup back on a saucer.

"No, but I daresay he will see to Mr. Bartley tomorrow. Lord Ridgeton offered us the use of his carriage, but there is nowhere I want to go," she added.

Emily giggled. "Mr. Wilkes would love to have the carriage at his disposal."

Arabella lifted her head and smiled, too. "I fear that would lead to panic on the part of the marquess."

"I daresay. He is used to an orderly, well-managed life."

"Yes." Arabella's own life, from the time her mother had died, had been eventful and full of changes. Clearly she and the marquess came from entirely different backgrounds. Yet when he had kissed her, she had felt a bond greater than the differences between them. Had he felt that?

"Would you like tea?" Emily asked. "I am practicing pouring."

"Yes, tea would be quite nice."

Arabella devoted her attention to Emily and pushed aside the marquess's foolish declaration they were to forget what had occurred between them. She did not think either of them could. She was not even sure she wished to. It was a compelling memory—even if it never happened again.

The next day, Lord Ridgeton rose early. He was full of resolve to get on with the business at hand. The sooner it was accomplished, the sooner he could return to London.

The pain in his hands was no longer so sharp,

but he still winced when he turned the doorknob to leave his room.

It took him the better part of the morning to deal with various town officials in order to secure Harry's release. Finally Lord Ridgeton was shown to a cramped row of cells. There a jailer fumbled with a bunch of keys for what seemed an interminable time. The marquess dragged some coins from his pocket and dropped them into a promptly outstretched hand. The man's luck at finding the proper key improved dramatically.

"Mr. Bartley is in the last cell," the jailer said, with an obsequious smile. "This way."

Their footsteps sounded hollow and ominous as they walked down a narrow corridor bordered by dank, fetid cells. To the right and left, Lord Ridgeton saw prisoners eyeing him suspiciously.

They stopped at the last cell and he peered inside. Harry lay sleeping with one arm draped off the cot touching the floor. He snored loudly.

The jailer banged his heavy keys against the metal bars. "You've company, man."

Harry raised himself slowly as the door opened and the marquess approached.

"Cedric!" He bounded off the cot with childlike abandon and flung his arms about his visitor's neck.

Lord Ridgeton knew in a single breath that Harry had bathed infrequently while confined. He tried to back away, but Harry refused to release him.

Clutching at the marquess's brown superfine sleeve, he shouted, "Damn, but I'm glad to see you. Knew you'd come. Knew you would." Harry reached to hug him again.

Stepping back quickly, the marquess replied, "I am gratified you are happy, but pray, Harry, do not overdo the welcome."

"Not overdo it? What balderdash! At least let me shake your hand." Harry grabbed and pumped.

Pain shot through Lord Ridgeton and he jerked his hand away.

"What's wrong?"

"Slight injury," he muttered, and deflected the conversation by asking, "how have you been treated?"

"Treated!" Harry's face turned red with indignation and he scowled over the marquess's shoulder toward the guard. "I've been fed and watered, if that is what you mean, but I have been treated like a common criminal. I've been locked up without benefit of a magistrate or solicitor. I intend to make these country fools pay for holding me like this. Me! With six thousand pounds a year."

"Harry—"

"I'll see the lot of them swinging from stout ropes before this is over."

"No, you won't."

Unhearing, Harry tramped about the small cell shaking his fist. "The very idea of holding me like a common thief until—" Harry ground to a halt and lunged forward to crush the marquess in another burly embrace. "There will be time later for revenge. Let me look at you. It's devilish good to see you."

"There will be no revenge," the marquess repeated firmly.

" 'Course there will be! You don't think I'm going to stand for this, do you?"

Lord Ridgeton's patience broke. "Listen to me, Harry. I have had a long and tiresome journey up here—only to learn you broke the latch of a back door and entered a mill in the middle of the night. Not my mill, but someone else's!"

Harry examined his toes. "I was only mistaken by a door or two."

"You didn't have to break into the mill anyway," he shouted. "You could have walked in the front door in broad daylight. It really put a cap on it to pick the wrong mill."

"Honest mistake." Harry scampered to change the subject. "It must have been boring to travel up here all by yourself."

"I did not come alone," he bit out.

"Well, the servants, of course, but that doesn't count."

"Miss Fairingdale accompanied me."

Harry looked him over slowly. "Ah, so that's the way of it, is it? Don't blame you in the least for taking an interest in her—as pert and pretty as she is. She doesn't possess a fortune, but that's nothing to you." Harry hesitated and frowned. "Your intentions toward her are honorable, aren't they, Cedric?"

"I have no feelings one way or the other toward Miss Fairingdale, you idiot. We own a business together in Manchester and that is why she came." If that was not entirely the truth, he was going to make it the truth. He intended to extinguish whatever inappropriate feelings he had for her. Common sense demanded that he do so.

"You mean you're not betrothed to her? Making such a long journey gives rather a bad appearance . . ."

"Harry, I never knew you to act like a dowager chaperon," he said sharply. "Miss Fairingdale has her companion with her and all is perfectly proper." No, the time alone in his room, the mouthfuls she had spooned to him—*and* the reckless kisses—had not been proper, but that was in the past.

Harry nodded. "Good, I like her and shouldn't

want to think of you causing her reputation harm. She's got spirit. She'd keep a husband well in line." He chuckled to himself.

"I intend to be a husband before long," he announced curtly, "but not to her."

"You're going to wed?"

"Yes. The time has come."

Harry peered at him. "You certainly show no joy at the prospect. Why not wait until next Season when your temper is better?"

"I've no wish to discuss the matter. Get your things and let's go," he directed tersely.

As Harry scurried around the room, he talked nonstop. "Is Miss Fairingdale here in regard to the mill?"

"Yes." Lord Ridgeton dreaded what he would find when they toured the mill tomorrow. Having seen the buildings that had burned, he realized Arabella had been right to be concerned. He had disregarded her warnings, and now he was going to have to admit his blindness. Humility was not one of his strengths; he did not look forward to the moment.

"Cedric? Why are you standing there? Let's be gone." Harry favored the jailer with a scorching look before marching out the door.

On the way home in the carriage, the marquess told Harry about events in London since his leaving. He also told about the fire in Manchester. He did not say how little he had slept last night—or relate the dream he had had concerning Arabella when he had slept.

Lord Ridgeton's illness left Arabella with time on her hands. Emily suggested browsing through the shops, but Arabella had a more productive plan. She would visit the mill with Sir David's list. That would give her the chance to make a thorough survey before she and Lord Ridgeton went to the mill together.

Arabella, Emily, and Mr. Wilkes headed out early in the day. Arabella wore a purple and lavender pelisse that would not have been stylish in London but that drew second glances here. Emily carried the stick with the bell in deference to Mr. Wilkes.

The threesome went in a hackney cab. Lord Ridgeton had already left with his carriage, undoubtedly to effect Harry's release.

After rambling through narrow streets bordered on either side by bleak buildings, and, after being halted for a few moments by a balking mule in the center of a street, they finally reached the wide wooden building that was the mill.

Arabella stepped through the front door and saw half a dozen surprised young women look up at her over the tops of whirling wooden machines. Mr. Wilkes went immediately to look at the equipment spinning out thread.

Emily moved in closer to Arabella. "It smells bad in here."

"Yes, the air is close."

"Are there windows? I can't feel any breeze."

Arabella looked at her sheet of paper and saw that was one of Sir David's questions. "There are a few windows, but they are closed."

A man flew into the room. He was round everywhere—from his chubby face, to his big stomach, to his stout legs. Even his fingers were like fat sausages. His hair was short and black and his cheeks apple red. "See here, what's the meaning of this? We are not a public house open for viewing." His gaze settled on Arabella. "Oh, it's you, Miss Fairingdale." There was no joy in his recognition.

"Yes, Mr. Daley. I wish to make an inspection of the mill."

The overseer rolled his eyes to the ceiling. "On my dear mother's grave, Miss Fairingdale, I wish you would leave matters to me. I've been managing this mill for over five years."

"That is what troubles me," she said crisply.

He heard the young women titter and swung around to glare at them.

"You needn't concern yourself with me, Mr. Daley. I shall show myself about," Arabella announced airily. "When I am through, I may wish to consult you on certain questions."

He looked back at her. "It is said Lord Ridgeton is in Manchester. Surely he and I could discuss matters more properly."

"The marquess intends to come to the mill. I," Arabella informed him, "am here now."

"Yes, I see," he grumbled.

From his position on his knees in the corner, Mr. Wilkes raised his head to announce, "This machine would run more efficiently if the wheels were larger and several spindles removed from it."

Mr. Daley jerked his head toward the inventor. "Who in blazes is he?"

"Mr. Wilkes is an authority on factory equipment. He will be making a thorough survey of the building." Arabella stepped past Mr. Daley. "Come along, Emily. This is only the first of several rooms on the main floor."

Emily tightened her grip on Arabella's elbow as they walked by a machine wheeling out thread. The next chamber was larger, but the presence of more machines and more people made it seem smaller. Arabella stopped to make notes about several children who stood dangerously close to the fast-moving parts.

It took the better part of an hour to inspect the entire building, including the upstairs. Arabella found Mr. Daley when she was done. "I should like to see a list of menus, so I shall know what the children eat."

He gaped at her.

"They are fed, are they not?" she demanded.

"Miss Fairingdale, we are not a fine establishment like the White Willow. The children are fed whatever the cook brings in that day."

"How can I be sure they are getting enough to eat or that the food is healthy?"

Mr. Daley appealed to the ceiling.

"The second floor isn't stout enough to hold all the equipment," Mr. Wilkes shouted down from the top of the stairs.

"Of course it is," Mr. Daley yelled back. He looked to Arabella. "Who did you say he was?"

She made a note that the machinery on the top floor was too heavy.

"What are you writing?" the overseer demanded.

"I am listing the problems." She glanced up at him. "These rooms are too small and narrow. If the fire that occurred the other night had happened here, lives might have been lost."

"It didn't happen here. We've never had the least trouble," he replied. "Some idiot did break into a building not far from here a couple of weeks ago, but I increased our locks after that. You couldn't get in here now no matter how hard you tried."

"Or out," she said, with a hard look at the bolts on the windows.

Before Mr. Daley could argue, she led Emily outside and they entered another hackney cab. Mr. Wilkes sat up front with the driver as they started back to the inn.

"Did it look dreadful?" Emily asked.

"Yes. Now that I have seen it a second time, I am more convinced than ever of the need for improvements. Lord Ridgeton will simply have to provide the funds."

"He was not inclined to do so before," Emily reminded her cautiously.

"We were strangers when I first applied to him for money. We know each other better now. I understand his character. He can be dogmatic and arrogant, but he can also be sensible and even caring." He could also be intense and passionate, but she was not going to dwell on that.

Emily reached for the strap as they sped around a corner. "He has been kindness itself to me. Still, work at the mill would require a great deal of money, would it not?"

"It would be a lot for me but little enough for him." Arabella looked out the window at the narrow, twisting street bordered on either side by shops with large signs hanging out front. She had never before hungered for money, but now she wondered what would have happened if she had been a wealthy debutante.

Would Lord Ridgeton have courted her? Would he have come to her house with flowers and pretty love notes? She smiled to herself at the notion of him laboring over a paper to find just the right word to rhyme. She laughed outright at the thought of him reading his poetry aloud.

"What is funny?" Emily asked as the cab hurtled around another corner. "It is surely not the driver. He is so reckless that I am beginning to feel ill."

"We'll be there soon." Arabella didn't bother to tell Emily about her ridiculous thoughts. She was not rich, and Lord Ridgeton had not courted her. Indeed, she would never see him again after they reached London.

She bit her lip at the thought.

They crested a hill and Arabella's stomach fluttered up into her throat. "Dear me, the driver is careless," she murmured, but was secretly glad to have somewhere else to fix her attention.

At dinnertime, Harry sat resplendent in a coat of ivory satin and breeches of chocolate brown. His face was already flushed from what appeared to be an afternoon of celebrating his release. He blazed a smile in her direction. "Miss Fairingdale, may I say you are looking lovely this evening," he declared.

"Thank you." Arabella touched the frilled edge of her scoop-necked *capucine* gown and smiled at the plump man. On the other side of the table, in the small but elegantly appointed room, Lord Ridgeton sat mute. He, like she, was unable to talk because Harry monopolized the conversation. She had twice tried to tell about going to the mill, but each time Harry had rolled over her words in a torrent of exuberant talk.

"It took eight men to subdue me and bring me out of the building. Eight."

The marquess reached for his glass and noted blandly, "A moment ago it was six, Harry."

"Six could not have done it."

Arabella caught the marquess's eye and they both smiled at Harry's bragging.

"It was a hard life in jail," Harry continued. "Newgate would not be any harder." The servants appeared with more dishes and Harry attacked his plate. "It's good to eat at last. I've been near to famished."

That was more than could be determined from his waistline, Arabella thought with amusement.

Between mouthfuls, Harry continued, "Your hands look bad, Cedric. It will surely be days before you can handle the ribbons." Without waiting for a reply, he quaffed some wine and swiveled toward Arabella. "And may I say, Miss Fairingdale, you look well. Such a long journey would have sent many young ladies to their chambers for days to recover, yet you are positively blooming. Isn't she, Cedric?"

"Miss Fairingdale always looks healthy." The marquess reached for his own glass of wine without looking toward her.

"Such a lukewarm compliment, Cedric," Harry chided. "Look at her complexion. Isn't it glowing?"

"You are forcing his lordship into praise he may not wish to give," Arabella demurred. She wondered if his lordship was acting distant to her so she would feel more comfortable with him. Yes, that must be it. This was his way of helping forget the kisses they had exchanged.

"Don't know why not," Harry hammered on. "Cedric has a way with pretty words when he wishes."

"Harry, how much wine have you had?" Lord Ridgeton inquired.

"Only a glass or two. My vision is still good. Besides, even when I'm dead drunk I know a pretty woman when I see one."

Arabella smiled at the lopsided compliment.

"Must have been a long trip from London, what?" Harry reached for more bread.

"The time passed quickly enough," the marquess said laconically. "We stopped to visit Sir William and stayed the night."

"Egad! In that monstrosity of a house. Shouldn't wonder if you didn't sleep at all."

"It was not so bad. He wants us to stop on our return trip."

"Send him a note that I'm already suffering from prison pallor and don't wish to worsen the condition by rattling about in that dungeon." Harry swung back to Arabella like a fat puppet on agile strings. "Have you been bored beyond reason with Cedric injured and you without an escort, Miss Fairingdale? Dreadful to be trapped like this. It makes it worse when another is in pain and there is nothing you can do."

Arabella lowered her gaze and examined the silver rim around her plate. She had done something. She had fed the marquess—and he had put his hands to the side of her face and kissed her. That did not, however, seem appropriate dinner-table conversation, especially not when Lord Ridgeton was trying to act as if they were nothing but casual acquaintances.

Harry got up from the table and paced around the room. Confinement had clearly made him restless. "I'm a bit stiff from sitting." Harry shot a wistful look toward the window. "I'll take a quick turn about outside and be back before you know I'm gone." He disappeared out the door before anyone could object.

Lord Ridgeton watched him go. "We shan't see him again tonight. I don't know whether that is good or bad," he added wrily.

"He has spent a long time locked away. This will give him a chance to release some of his restlessness."

"I only hope he does not fall into any further scrapes," Lord Ridgeton muttered.

"I'm sure he's learned his lesson."

The marquess lifted one dark eyebrow in disbelief and she laughed. "You may be right. Did it cost a great deal to get him released?"

"Yes." The taut line of his mouth quirked upward in a mean smile. "However, as you are fond of reminding me, I am as rich as a nabob."

"I never said that! Well," she admitted when he contradicted her with a pointed look, "I was only direct in discussing funds with regard to the mill." It was clearer than ever that his money would be needed, but now did not seem the moment to broach the subject. In truth, Arabella was having a difficult time defining his attitude toward her. He acted courteously distant, but she thought his glances toward her betrayed a keener interest.

"Direct?" The eyebrow came into play again. "Miss Fairingdale, you stormed my study and listed your demands as if you were a requisition officer and I a lowly foot soldier."

"I was only insistent because you were so unhelpful."

"I saw no reason to be helpful," he said bluntly. "I wanted you to leave."

If she had left that first day and given up in defeat, they would not have come to Manchester. Not only would she have lost the hope of seeing the mill improved, but she would never have glimpsed the gentler soul beneath his arrogant exterior. He was not at present showing that gentler soul, she noted.

Arabella ignored that and said matter-of-factly, "It has all worked out for the best. You are here, and tomorrow we shall visit the mill. I think you will agree with my assessments."

He did not reply and Arabella did not press. Instead, she asked, "Are your hands improved?"

"Yes."

"You never wore Mr. Wilkes's gloves."

"No, I did not wish to make a fool of myself."

"It would have pleased him," she scolded gently. "And it might have eased your discomfort."

"I shall try his next invention."

She burst into laughter. "Mr. Wilkes is perfecting a woman's corset."

"Dear me," he drawled. "His interests seem quite varied."

"Yes. It is what keeps him young." Wickedly she pressed, "Does your offer to try his next invention stand good?"

"I think not."

He was leaning back in his chair and looking at her from beneath half-closed eyes. He was surely no more handsome today than he had been yesterday, but firelight and easy conversation made him particularly appealing. Arabella almost wished he were sick again, so she would have an excuse to touch him, to brush back the hair from his forehead, to drop a soft kiss on his cheek.

"What of Mr. Wilkes's other inventions?" he asked. "Do you ride about in his carriage just to please him?"

"Yes."

He chuckled low in his throat and shook his head in wonder. "Each time I think I understand you, you change. First, you are a plainspoken woman intent on having your own way, then you turn into a lady willing to inconvenience yourself to spare someone's feelings."

"Well, no one is the same all the time. That would be boring."

"Some would call it being consistent."

Arabella dismissed that with a shake of her head. "I have always found the most interesting people to be unpredictable."

"Mmmm." He tilted the wineglass toward his lips and watched her over the dark liquid through even darker eyes.

In the silence that fell between them, she heard the enamel clock ticking on the mantel. They had been here long enough by themselves. Pushing back her chair, she said, "It is late and time to retire to my room."

He stood politely. "Good night."

She did not really want to go to bed, though. She was not yet tired and she wanted to think. She left the inn through a side door and stepped into the garden. The low hedges were kissed with an iridescent glow from a silver moon. Light and shadow intertwined among the rosebushes.

She inhaled the fragrance of the roses and turned her face up toward the glowing moon.

"Nice, ain't it?" a man's voice asked.

She pivoted to find Harry smiling at her.

"Yes. I thought you had left." Or at least she hoped he *would* leave, so she could have time alone.

"I came back to see about Cedric." Harry dropped his voice and weaved to the side. "I'm concerned about him. He is not the man he used to be. 'Course, I've changed, too, since being confined. Indeed, I've become a different person. I daresay you've noticed." He paused to give her the opportunity to press him for information about his transformation.

Instead she asked, "Why is Lord Ridgeton not the man he used to be?"

Harry took her arm and began leading her down a path strewn with rose petals and moonbeams. "He told me some outrageous tale about buying fighting chickens—cocks, if you will—and shipping them to his estate, so they wouldn't be killed." He blinked at her owlishly. "Have you ever heard of anything so peculiar? He also told me he didn't enjoy London and said it seemed meaningless to attend the auctions at Tattersall's. Meaningless! One of the finest horse auctions in the country. Well, you must see that something is wrong."

Nothing Harry had said signaled that Lord

Ridgeton had gone mad. Arabella thought the marquess had merely matured while Harry remained full of youthful abandon. She was on the point of saying so when he continued.

"It's Cedric's sudden decision to marry that I cannot like."

"Marry?" She stopped and faced him.

"Yes. Every man is obliged to take a wife sooner or later. I trust I do not offend your sensibilities by pointing out that most men find more excitement outside marriage than within."

She stared at him. "The marquess is engaged to wed?" Why had he said nothing to her?

"He is not yet engaged, but he will be soon. He could have his pick, of course. Can't recall which chit he said it would be." Harry frowned. "Maybe he didn't say."

She felt a sinking sensation, like the time she had fallen from the loft. Married. Some other woman would sit beside him in his exquisitely sprung carriage. He would escort another woman to the balls and fetes in London. Another woman would be the mistress of his house in Salisbury. Arabella had never thought she would be the marquess's wife, but she did admit to having formed a foolish attachment to him. Now he was to marry another. She was aware of a blind need to get away.

Harry stumbled against a stone wall, righted himself, and peered at her in the uneven light. "Is something wrong, Miss Fairingdale?"

"I'm chilled," she said over the thickness in her throat. "I wish to go back into the inn."

"We haven't walked long," Harry protested.

"I want to go back immediately." She longed to close the door of her room behind her, sink into a chair, and reason her way out of feeling lost and unhappy.

"Well, of course." They turned and started back. "Thing is, Cedric—"

"Mr. Bartley"—Arabella cut him off sharply—"I would rather not discuss Lord Ridgeton's personal affairs." Not when talking about them cut at her like knives and left her forsaken and woebegone.

He shrugged. "I thought you would want to know. I fancied you liked Cedric and considered him a friend. Well," he confessed, "I *did* think he might have other arrangements in mind for you, but I see now I was wrong about that."

She stopped outside the door and asked hollowly, "Other arrangements?"

"Don't mean to offend you, but it stands to reason any man would look at you and want you. You're pretty and you have a saucy manner and fetching smile. Sometimes instead of marriage a man . . . er . . . considers other options."

"Oh!" She wrapped her shawl defensively around her, as if by doing so she could ward off his words. She started toward the door.

Harry followed on her heels. "Cedric's not a monk, you know. I'll warrant he has noticed you with more than a passing interest. Well, he has as much as said so, but he did say he would not marry you."

"Oh," she gasped as she fumbled for the door handle. "This is insulting. I do not wish to hear any more."

"You are right. It was ill said of me. I'm certain Cedric never looked at you in any but the purest lights. Hasn't given you any jewelry, has he? He gives emeralds to his ladybirds. Forgive me, it's the wine talking. Pray don't attend anything I say."

Arabella yanked the door open and fled to her room.

She had been excessively foolish, she upbraided

herself. Lord Ridgeton had warned her to disregard his kisses. Now he was to marry someone else and she was behaving like a peagoose.

By the time she reached the door of her room, she was angry with him as well as herself. He should not have kissed her when he knew he had no real interest in her. He should not have looked at her with those dark eyes. And he should not have been such pleasant company during the journey.

Chapter 10

THE MOMENT Lord Ridgeton saw Arabella the next day, he knew something was wrong. She must be worried about what they would find at the mill. Why else did she greet him so stiffly? Her face was pale beneath a dark little bonnet. He even imagined she shrank away from him when he handed her up into the carriage. Once seated inside, she sat with poker stiffness.

He tried to reassure her. "This won't take long, I promise you," he said gently.

When she looked at him, he thought something bitter glittered in her eyes. Turning, she stared out the window as raptly as if Manchester was the most beautiful town in the world instead of a cramped, dark mill village.

Was this her way of punishing him because he had not listened to her warnings about the mill? He did not know why she should show her anger now, when she had not before, but there was no understanding women.

They were halfway across town when she took a deep breath and turned to face him. "Harry says you mean to choose a wife."

Blast Harry. He had not intended for the idiot to tell the whole world.

Her skewering gaze made it impossible to look away. Well, he had nothing to hide. He had a right to wed whomever he chose, when he chose, and he was not going to be intimidated by those chilly blue eyes. "Yes," he said in clipped tones.

"Why didn't you tell me?" Her gaze remained cold, but he thought her voice wavered briefly.

He hesitated. Was she overset at the thought of him marrying or merely annoyed that he had not told her? "It did not seem necessary to tell you."

"Not even when you were kissing me?" she asked faintly.

She had no right to make him feel guilty. He had apologized for kissing her. She was the one who had made too much of that embrace. Drawing himself up with stern dignity, he reminded her, "We agreed from the beginning our purpose for coming here involved the mill. I saw no reason to inform you of something that had nothing to do with the mill." Nor had there ever been a time when it would have felt comfortable to do so. She was right; he could hardly have made such an announcement while he was bestowing kisses on her.

She looked at him with wide, accusing eyes.

He disliked being made to feel uncomfortable. "We shall arrive at the mill momentarily," he said shortly. "We should concentrate on that instead of on recriminations over something I did or did not tell you."

Her head came up higher and her mouth tightened into a defiant line before she turned to look out the opposite window.

Lord Ridgeton stared out his own window and reflected what a mull Harry had made of matters. Very well, it had not been solely Harry. The marquess himself had taken unwarranted liberties with Arabella, but that he could not change and had resolved never to do again.

"We are here," she pronounced in icy accents.

He stepped out, handed Arabella down, and followed her to the doorway. The front door opened and a burly man in a too small brown coat flew out.

The man greeted them with a delighted smile and a bow so low his head nearly scraped the sidewalk. "Lord Ridgeton. I am Adam Daley, the overseer. I am most pleased to meet you, milord." He followed with another bow.

"Hello, Mr. Daley," Arabella said. The icy Thames could never have been colder.

The overseer nodded but kept his gaze on the marquess. "I do hope the day finds you well, milord?"

"Yes."

"We wish to go inside, Mr. Daley," Arabella said curtly, and suited her actions to her words.

Lord Ridgeton followed her into a small crowded room where young women stood shoulder-to-shoulder working machinery that stood taller than he. The equipment hummed and spun and drew continuous lines of thread through it. The air was heavy with the odor of chemicals and unbathed bodies—and something acrid he could not define. The windows were small and did not let in enough light. It was indeed as bad as Arabella had said.

He did not look forward to admitting he had been wrong, especially not while she was in her present mood. This was going to be a long day.

Beaming, Mr. Daley pointed about with a hickory cane. "Modern, as you can see. We have the latest machines. We're not using any of Samuel Crompton's outmoded mule machinery; indeed, we are not. We've Cartwright looms with upright warps."

All that meant little to him, but some things were clear. "The room is small," Lord Ridgeton observed. The women's arms nudged one another as they reached forward to make adjustments to machines and add more thread.

The overseer waved the cane dismissingly. "Don't worry about that. Haven't had more than one or two a week grow faint from lack of air. It's usually the younger ones, and they're easily revived."

Arabella's eyes widened with horror. Mr. Daley blithely ignored her and led them through a welter of small rooms. The marquess remembered the conflagration and the sight of blazing walls collapsing. If a fire occurred here, dozens of people would be trapped and die.

"Have you ever had a fire, Mr. Daley?" he asked.

"Nothing to speak of."

Arabella whirled to stare at him. "You said yesterday you never had."

He shrugged thick shoulders. "Only a small one."

"Are the doors kept unlocked during work hours?" Lord Ridgeton asked.

"Can't do that, now can we?" Smiling, the overseer leaned close to him. "I'd have the younger ones slipping out to play and the older ones scooting out when they pleased. We run a business here. Have to keep 'em working or we don't make a profit."

"Most of the children don't look like they have the energy to play," Arabella said. "How much time are they given at leisure each day?"

"They have an hour and a half at lunch. All the time in the world. They've got it soft, our workers have." He turned away from her.

"They are here at six in the morning and they don't go home until eight in the evening, yet they only receive one meal?" Arabella pursued.

Mr. Daley's smile was as strained as the buttons on his coarse cloth coat. "Yes. Just like all the other mills."

"We don't want to be like the others, Mr. Daley,"

she declared, and put her hands emphatically on her hips. "We want to be better."

The overseer looked at her as if she had just said she wanted to teach the workers to spin cotton into gold. "We can't do that."

"Of course we can. Surely you have heard of Mr. Robert Owen?"

"A revolutionary idiot." Mr. Daley appealed to the marquess for support. "You don't expect me to run this like a charity, do you, milord?"

"I think changes must be made," Lord Ridgeton said. Large changes. His man of business would have to survey the equipment and mill before they could decide what must be changed and how quickly.

He looked toward Arabella and saw that she glared at him as if he were as callous and unfeeling as Adam Daley. Devil take it! What did she want? He had agreed changes were warranted. Wasn't that what she had wished for all along?

"I should like to see the upper floors." Arabella swept up her gray skirts in angry preparation for climbing the stairs.

The overseer looked toward Lord Ridgeton for permission.

"If she wishes."

"I do wish!"

The woman was in rare form today. Lord Ridgeton watched her warily as they toured the cramped upper floors. Arabella asked a few questions and Mr. Daley answered with an air of martyred patience.

Once they were alone in the carriage, she turned to him belligerently. "See, it is as bad as I told you!"

He tried for a calming tone. "Why are you speaking to me as if I am the enemy, Arabella? We must work together for a solution."

"That solution will require a great deal of money," she said flatly. "Will you put money into the mill?"

"I intend to do so," he muttered.

"Splendid." She turned away.

"A little gratitude would be welcome." At the very least she could have thanked him. Ungrateful wench.

She flipped a look over her shoulder at him. "Gratitude because you have agreed to fulfill your obligations?" she inquired sarcastically.

He saw there was nothing to be gained by talking to her. He folded his arms across his chest and sat back irritably. If she thought he was going to grovel and apologize, he was not.

They drove back to the inn in silence.

Emily was in the sitting room when Arabella returned. "Well," she asked from her chair by the window, "did Lord Ridgeton agree with your assessments?"

"Yes." Arabella felt tired and defeated even though she had won a victory.

"When shall we leave to go back to London?" Emily asked, with an edge of impatience.

"I have decided to remain here for a time." Arabella pulled off her gloves and flipped them against her open palm as she stared into the empty fire grate. It had been a most unpleasant day—made worse by the fact her anger did not entirely blunt a greater pain within.

"That will delay the marquess's journey back," Emily noted.

Arabella took a deep breath and shook her head. "No. I shall insist he leave without us. We can return later on the stage." Her funds would not allow them to remain overlong, but she had enough to last a week or two. If they found cheaper lodging, they could stretch that even further.

"Oh?"

Ignoring the unspoken questions in Emily's voice,

Arabella pulled her pelisse from her shoulders. She was concerned about the workers, but she also did not want to travel in a closed carriage with Lord Ridgeton for several days. She did not wish to sit across from him and speculate about the woman he would marry.

On impulse Arabella swung the pelisse back over her shoulders and started toward the door. She was too restless to sit inside. She wanted to be by herself and reason away this unsuitable *tendre* she had formed toward the marquess. She told herself it should not be so hard to get over him after the way he had acted toward her today.

"I believe I shall go for a turn about the garden to clear my head, Emily."

"Do you want me to accompany you?"

"No. I shan't be long."

Arabella had just left her room when she almost collided with Harry. He jumped out of the way, stumbled backward, and fell to the floor with a graceless thud.

"Are you all right?" She knew she should have sounded more sympathetic, but the last thing she wished right now was to deal with Harry.

He got slowly to his feet and rubbed at his backside. "I have endured far worse. I daresay I shall recover."

"Good." She started to leave.

He blocked her path. "Miss Fairingdale, didn't you stay with Lady Hector in London?"

"Yes," she said unencouragingly.

"I met someone last night who is acquainted with her. Well, he doesn't know her now," Harry clarified. "He knew her many years ago, before she married."

"How nice." With a dismissing smile, she took a step toward him, forcing him to move to the side of the hall.

"Knew her quite well, I gather. He was connected

with the Windlemeres, and his family lived not far from where she grew up."

Arabella stopped inches from Harry. The man with whom Lady Hector had planned to run away to Gretna Green had such connections. Had Harry Bartley found the countess's long-lost love? "Where did you meet this man?"

"Last night over a game of cards. He ships textiles to the Continent. Even though he has made his blunt in trade, he seemed an amiable sort."

For a blind moment, Arabella grasped at the idea of reuniting Lady Hector with the man from her youth. A more practical side warned her he was probably married and his youthful passion in ashes. It was best to forget Harry had ever said anything. She shot him a bright smile and murmured a word of parting. She had enough things to occupy her mind already.

In the garden, she stalked up and down the paths hoping to calm herself by sheer physical activity. Her thoughts continued to dart about wildly. She remembered Lord Ridgeton's reserve when she had first met him, and she recalled the more relaxed moments that had passed between them in Sir William's stables in the middle of the night. She thought of kisses and glances and the hole that had been torn in her world when Harry had told her the marquess was to wed.

Sighing, she slowed and looked up at the cloudless sky. Would she really get over this disappointment? Look at Lady Hector; she still loved a man who had been gone from her life over thirty years.

Arabella rubbed her temples and sank down onto a stone bench. A gardener clipped hedges nearby, making a loud, slicing noise that helped bring her back to reality. She straightened and reminded herself she had come to Manchester to help the workers at the mill. She must apply herself to that end and forget everything else.

Hadn't she known all along Lord Ridgeton would marry at some time? Men in his position were bound to. She had also known he would select a woman of impeccable breeding who came with a large dowry and a meek mien.

"I possess neither," she declared aloud.

The gardener looked over at her. "Did you say something, miss?"

"Nothing worth hearing."

He looked at her narrowly.

Rising, she started to her rooms. She fought back the cowardly urge to send a note saying she would not join the men for dinner. She must go and explain to Lord Ridgeton that she intended to remain in Manchester. After that, she need have no further intercourse with him.

Up in her room, Emily assisted her into a stern gray dress with a stiff white fichu collar. Arabella's nerves grew more frayed as the time for dinner approached. She turned to her companion and said impulsively, "Join me for dinner, Emily. It seems a shame that you always dine alone."

Emily bit her lip. "I do not know if I am ready to eat with others."

"I need you there," Arabella said quietly. She had not realized until this moment how much she both longed for and dreaded seeing the marquess. It would help to have her companion beside her.

"Is something wrong?" Emily asked in quick concern.

"It is only that I am confused. My thoughts are on the mill, you understand, but Lord Ridgeton is to wed, and . . . I am unhappy at the notion of him spending his life with another. I did not think he would spend his life with me, of course, but we had sometimes come to deal well together . . ." Her words faded away again. "At any rate, I wish you would join us for dinner."

Emily nodded as if Arabella's jumbled sentences made perfect sense. "Of course I shall accompany you. I daresay I can eat as neatly as Mr. Bartley can."

Arabella smiled.

At dinner, Lord Ridgeton greeted Arabella politely and she returned a distant greeting.

Once they were seated, she took a deep breath and began, "Milord, I do not wish to prevent you from leaving Manchester whenever you are ready. I, however, intend to remain here." She wished his bourbon brown eyes did not look at her with such piercing thoroughness.

"Why?" he demanded.

"I can be present when your man of business arrives," she said briskly. "Until then I shall tour some of the other mills and investigate those that are more progressive. I shall talk to other millowners."

He laid down his knife in exasperation. "Do not be addlepated. I cannot go off and leave you alone."

"I shan't be alone. Emily and Mr. Wilkes will be with me."

He glanced toward her blind companion; Arabella knew he wanted to object but could not with Emily present. "We shall discuss this later," he said.

"There is nothing to discuss," she countered. "I have made my decision."

"Arabella," he snapped, "I trust you are not going to be as stubborn about this as you have shown yourself to be about everything else!"

"See here, Cedric. If she wishes to stay, that is her decision. I," Harry continued as he scooped asparagus onto a fork, "stand ready to leave tomorrow. I have missed enough of the Season as it is."

The marquess looked at him as if he were a bothersome fly. "The Season will be over by the time we reach London, Harry."

"What of your mother's house party? I shouldn't want to be late for it. *You* certainly cannot be late. The women are probably already flocking to your estate."

Arabella swallowed back a heavy lump. Of course they were. No doubt the marquess would be engaged within a week after reaching his home. "Then it is settled," she said. "You are free to leave tomorrow and I shall remain here."

She blinked rapidly to clear her eyes of tears. It was foolish to be so emotional, and she was glad Lord Ridgeton did not notice. Only Emily seemed to sense her unhappiness and leaned over to touch her arm gently.

Lord Ridgeton and his party left the following morning just as the sky was growing bold with sunshine and the horses stamping with impatience to be away.

He sat brooding in the corner of the carriage. As the morning ground on, the only sound inside the carriage was Harry's incessant chatter. Outside, the relentless noise of the wheels seemed to hammer out a warning, but he could not decipher its meaning.

"Are you worried about Miss Fairingdale?" Harry asked during a lull in his own conversation about the miserable conditions of prison life.

"I am not happy with the notion of leaving her behind." Nor was he happy with the tension that had existed between them last night at dinner. Her eyes had seemed like hard blue crystals, but once he thought he had detected the sheen of tears in them. At that moment, he had felt a doubt that reached deep into him.

"I daresay her remaining in Manchester is better

than going to Kent to live on Lord Seagraves's estate," Harry said cheerfully.

He turned to stare at his companion. "I did not know she lived on his property."

"Goodness, yes. I suspect it is the only place she can afford. Still, you must know the rumors surrounding Seagraves."

He knew all too well. Moodily he stared down at his boots. He had tried to warn Arabella about the earl, but she had resisted his suggestions. It had never occurred to him she might be dependent on Lord Seagraves. This was indeed a bad turn of events.

What to do? he wondered as Harry sank off to sleep on the seat across from him.

What to do indeed?

The question went from a gentle nagging to an insistent screech in his mind as the wheels continued to churn beneath him. He had left Arabella in Manchester with an undependable older man and a blind woman to protect her. What had he been thinking? Even worse, when she did remove to Kent, she would be venturing inside the spider's web. Could he in good conscience allow her to live on Lord Seagraves's property?

The idea plagued him for the next five miles. Other, less easily answered questions, circled like birds of prey. He had not known he would begin missing Arabella the moment they pulled away from the inn. He had not known he would feel bleak and taciturn at the knowledge he would never see her again.

The wheels continued turning, carrying him further and further away from her.

What if he was doing the wrong thing? He was not accustomed to doubting himself and his decisions. The uncertainty gnawed at him.

Abruptly he pulled on the rope and the driver halted. Lord Ridgeton put his head out the window.

"We are going back to Manchester." Charles, who sat beside Harry, looked at him in astonishment.

"Did we leave something, milord?"

"Yes," he barked.

Charles subsided into silence, no doubt discouraged by Lord Ridgeton's tone.

They were passing through the sleepy hamlet of Grove Park when Harry roused himself and mumbled, "Where are we?"

"Grove Park."

Blinking, the stout man sat up straighter. "We passed through here this morning. Is your driver lost?"

"No. I have decided to return to Manchester."

"Why?" Harry bleated.

"It was wrong to abandon Miss Fairingdale."

"You didn't abandon her. God's teeth, she wanted you to leave. Judging from the way she looked at you last night at dinner, she doesn't even like you, Cedric. Certainly when I spoke with her in the garden, she did not give the impression she is your friend."

"Shut up, Harry." He was fighting enough doubts of his own. He did not need any more.

"I'm only trying to help. Besides, I want to go back to civilization. When I came to investigate, I didn't intend to spend the rest of my life in Manchester."

"Harry, it was because of you that I was obliged to come to Manchester in the first place," he snarled.

"Honest mistake. It could have happened to anyone. I may not be the best investigator, but I try. I know I wasn't able to recover the Saxharts' silver, but I did locate *some* stolen silver. It was far better than what had been taken from them, and they were very grateful. As far as being in the wrong mill, that could have happened to anyone."

Lord Ridgeton forebore to comment.

"It seems a shame to miss the last days of the Season," Harry complained.

"I can put you down at the next coaching stop, but Charles and I are returning to Manchester."

"Then I shall return with you," Harry declared in long-suffering accents. "You may need me."

With that unlikely suggestion hanging in the air, Lord Ridgeton crossed his arms and sat staring across at the thick velvet cushions.

"What of your mother's house party?" Harry roused himself to ask. "You cannot be late for that."

"I shall send her a note."

"A note! Cedric, she has gathered women for your inspection. She expects you to come and do the pretty by them. Lud, Cedric, she expects you to choose a bride—and you said you were ready. Have to have an heir, now don't you? Women may be troublesome, but I know of no man who has been able to produce an heir without the aid of one.

"Not such an onerous task to beget a child," Harry continued, staring at the roof of the carriage and following his own line of thought. "Once you have a son, you need not spend any time with your wife."

"If I had a wife, I would spend time with her," Lord Ridgeton declared.

Harry shook his head mournfully. "Cedric, I'm deeply concerned about you. First you bought those cocks and now you are talking foolishness about spending time with a wife. You need a long rest. Manchester is not the place to rest," Harry added. "I hope you can persuade Miss Fairingdale to return southward quickly. 'Course persuading her of anything is difficult. She's pretty but she's headstrong."

The marquess smiled wrily. Yes, she was headstrong, but he was not going to allow her to fall into Seagraves's lecherous clutches. What exactly he intended to do to prevent that, he did not yet know. It would be no simple task to approach Arabella—not now when she seemed so prickly and defiant, but he would think of something.

Arabella, Mr. Wilkes, and Emily toured two mills before noon. The first overseer had been surprised but polite. The second one had looked at her askance, but when Mr. Wilkes began surveying the machinery, the overseer had proudly shown off his equipment.

Shortly after noon, the little party returned to the inn in a hackney cab. Mr. Wilkes sat up front with the driver.

"It's not so elegant as Lord Ridgeton's carriage, is it?" Emily asked from a dark corner as they jolted along.

"No, but it is not as bad as our own carriage that Mr. Wilkes devised."

"True enough."

They both laughed. "I should not make fun of him," Arabella said guiltily. Still, laughing helped her forget the heaviness she had felt this morning when the marquess drove away. She had not gone out to wish him a safe journey or bid him farewell. Now he had departed; she doubted she would ever see him again.

"What do you mean to do this afternoon?" Emily asked.

"We shall rest and eat and then go back to tour another mill or two. Tomorrow I shall contact some of the people Sir David recommended." If she kept busy enough she would not have time for other thoughts.

"I am glad we don't have to move from our rooms.

Lord Ridgeton was kind to pay at the inn as long as we wish to stay."

"Yes." This morning when Arabella had approached the innkeeper about moving to smaller, less expensive rooms, he had told her the marquess had arranged everything.

"Of course, the marquess has a lot of money and can afford to be generous," Emily added.

Arabella smiled with a touch of sadness. "I have told him that myself. He did not appreciate it." Sighing, she looked out the window. "He and I seemed to cross swords at every turn." Yet somehow their differences did not loom so large in her mind as they once had.

"I thought you were coming to deal with each other better," Emily said.

"Some times were easier than others." A carriage rolled by in front of her and Arabella thought she saw Lord Ridgeton's swirling crest. Good heavens, she was thinking of him so much she was even conjuring him up. "It is better that he is gone," she said stoutly. "Now I can concentrate on the mill."

Emily nodded as they swung around a corner and bounced about like unsecured boats in quick water. "I am getting queasy again. Are we nearly there?"

Arabella looked out the window and saw the inn. In front of it, looking very lifelike, was the same phantom carriage she had seen a moment ago. "It can't be," she murmured.

"We aren't almost there?" Emily's voice turned to a wail. "Oh, dear. I am going to be sick."

The cab darted around a slow-moving wagon, tossing the occupants from one corner to the other. Emily's face went green. Arabella pulled a handkerchief from her reticule and thrust it at her companion. "You'll be all right." She was too intent on staring out the window to offer further comfort.

Behind her, Emily gagged. In front of Arabella, the carriage door opened and a heavy man jumped down.

"Harry!" she said, breathing rapidly.

Then Charles alighted—and finally Lord Ridgeton. She blinked; this was no dream. There was no mistaking the marquess's purposeful stride or the way he held himself with such confidence. Heavens, but he looked good.

"Why have they returned?" Arabella wondered in a dazed voice.

"Make him stop the cab," Emily said faintly.

They lurched to a halt a moment later and Emily grasped at Arabella's hand. "Promise me we shall find another driver this afternoon."

"Emily, Lord Ridgeton has returned." Arabella barely noticed that the cabdriver had jumped down and stood holding the door open.

"Excellent. We can travel in his carriage."

"Why has he come back?" Arabella asked. Hopes fluttered and dived within her. She must not make too much of this, she warned herself.

Emily kept the handkerchief pressed against her mouth. "Aren't we getting out?"

"Yes, yes, of course." Arabella paused to adjust her dark blue bonnet and brush specks of dust from her pelisse before sliding down from the cab.

The marquess was starting toward the inn.

"Lord Ridgeton," she called in voice not quite her own.

He turned back.

A smile trembled on her lips. His caped coat was dusty from the road and his cravat was limp, but when he smiled at her she thought he looked glorious.

"Hello, Arabella."

"We have been out," she said unnecessarily as

he strode toward her. She took a breath. "I was not expecting you to return."

He did not address that statement; the hope soaring within began to plummet. His smile had also died, although he regarded her with steady intensity. "Let us go inside," he said. "I have not eaten and we can talk more comfortably over a meal."

But when Arabella joined his lordship in the small parlor, Harry was not present. What was more, Lord Ridgeton turned to Emily and said, "I have arranged to have a tray sent to your room, Miss Windell, so Miss Fairingdale and I may speak in private. I hope you do not object."

"No, of course not."

As the door closed behind Emily, Arabella sat slowly down and searched his face. Did his expression really soften when he looked at her or did she see what she wanted to see?

He put his fingertips together and said, "I came back because I have changed my mind."

"About the mill?" she asked unevenly. That would be a terrible blow, but—heaven help her—she was still glad to see him.

"It has nothing to do with the mill, Arabella."

She pressed her hands against the bottom of the chair to keep them from trembling and waited.

"I had time to think while I was on the road. I decided some things about both of us." He spread his hands apart and watched her.

Her breathing stopped and started undependably. "What sort of things?" she managed.

"I feared for your future with Lord Seagraves and—" He broke off with an impatient shake of his head. "That is not the truth. I feared for my own future without you. You see, I have concluded that I am not indifferent to you."

She wet her bottom lip with her tongue.

He leaned toward her, holding her captive with his gaze. "I have never before had difficulty expressing myself to women. The words have always rolled easily off my tongue, but they were glib, insincere phrases. I am suddenly without the right words."

He was silent so long she began to fear he was not going to finish. "You could try the glib phrases," she finally murmured. "If you say them with enough conviction I shall believe you."

"You're beautiful," he said solemnly.

She listened raptly. "I—I think you're very convincing."

"My feelings for you have grown stronger and stronger with the passing of time."

"That's very pretty." Arabella felt as if she were falling into the dark pools of his eyes. They seemed to beckon with promise even while his words fell from his lips and brushed across her like soft feathers.

"Arabella . . ." He rose and pushed back his chair.

She released her grip on the bottom of her chair and allowed him to pull her upward until they were standing close together.

"I came back because I could not bear being away from you."

She pressed her face against his shoulder and shuddered with relief and anticipation. "I am glad. I missed you dreadfully."

His breath blew across her cheeks. "I always thought I would take a wife only to produce an heir, but now I want a woman I can hold at night and laugh with in the sunshine. I want you, Arabella."

His lips traced across her cheek to hover near her mouth.

She could endure no more. Turning her head fractionally, she touched his lips. That seemed to be all the incentive he needed. He pulled her against him until every inch of her seemed poised to melt into him. As she pressed her palms into the wall of his chest, his lips captured hers. His mouth hovered and swirled over hers before pulling her slowly and deliberately into a deep vortex of a kiss. It was a delicious way to drown, she thought with dazed contentment.

She wondered then how she had thought she would exist without him if he had not returned. His embrace seemed necessary to her very survival.

The door opened and Harry swung in. "I was going to— See here, Cedric. What's the meaning of this? You told me before you wouldn't compromise Miss Fairingdale—yet here you are taking advantage of her. Ought to call you out," he grumbled.

"Go away, Harry."

"It's quite all right, Mr. Bartley," Arabella said breathlessly. "I believe Lord Ridgeton intends to propose marriage to me."

"Will you accept?" the marquess asked thickly.

His lips were close to her ear, and when he spoke she felt the most marvelous sensation rush through her.

"Marriage! What of the chits massed in Salisbury waiting for you? Your mother will not be pleased."

"I think she will." The marquess looked fondly down at Arabella and she preened shamelessly.

"You're not just doing this to save her from Seagraves, are you? Drastic step that would be."

"I am marrying Miss Fairingdale because I wish to. Get out."

"I shall," he declared in wounded accents, "but I wanted to tell you Lady Hector's old friend would like to contact her. Do you think that would be wise, Miss Fairingdale?"

"I think it would be lovely. And very romantic," she added dreamily.

"Go away, Harry."

Harry shut the door with a graceless thud.

Lord Ridgeton looked back down at her. "There are other reasons for wanting to marry you," he said quickly. "When I returned from the Continent, nothing mattered to me. I didn't care about the London social life or sports or gambling, but I came to care very much about you."

She stroked the fine linen of his cravat and looked shyly up at him.

"Come now, my girl." He shook her gently. "You're not going to be coy with me after all these days of speaking your mind freely."

She sighed and snuggled closer to him. "I do feel rather girlish and uncertain, but I shall recover."

He chuckled. "I hope you will. I'll not have a woman who simpers."

"I shall still wish to see things done right at the mill," she warned.

"I know."

"And Emily and Mr. Wilkes must be welcome in your household."

"He cannot tinker on my carriage."

"We can discuss that later." She lifted her mouth for another kiss. "As long as we are alone, we might as well make the best of the situation."

He started to kiss her, then drew back and surveyed her through dark, somber eyes. "What did you mean to do if I did not return?"

"Grieve," she said simply. "Perhaps for my whole life."

He pulled her back against him. "We're both rather stubborn and foolish, Arabella."

"Yes. We must endeavor to be less so." She ran her hand down the side of his cheek. His skin was smooth at the top while tiny bristles poked through on his lower cheek. It was an utterly masculine feel, and she found it satisfying to know she could touch him whenever she wished.

"I'll not have you grieving," he said in a quiet, determined voice. "I shall do my best to make you happy."

She looked back into his eyes and saw the promise there. Additional words seemed wholly without merit. She wanted to indulge herself in kisses and feel his strong hands on her back—and decide how she wished to redecorate his mansion.